PUFFIN BOOKS

Editor: Kaye Webb

PROFESSOR BRANESTAWM UP THE POLE

'Right,' said the Professor, getting all brisk and practical. He shot into his inventory, and with a cookery book in one hand, a spanner in the other and a wooden spoon behind his ear, he started inventing. The result was a fabulous, automatic, self-propelled, double reciprocating, sprocket-geared cake-making machine, so simple it almost worked itself. But the one thing it *hadn't* got was a safety switch to cut it out when Mrs Flittersnoop, the Professor's housekeeper, couldn't turn it off, and the cakes began whizzing through windows and attacking rescuers . . .

But an inventor of Professor Branestawm's calibre learns not to take setbacks too seriously, and maybe even to put them to good account. However many desperate situations his good friend Colonel Dedshott had to rescue him from, the Professor's mind still teemed anew with brilliantly simple ideas like his highly novel flagpole-painting machine, the picture-making machine, his prizewinning horse-powered boat, and the railway which gave him the signal distinction of achieving a collision though using only one train.

Professor Branestawm and his remarkable ideas are celebrated in three other Puffin books, *The Incredible Adventures of Professor Branestawm*, *Professor Branestawm's Treasure Hunt* and *The Peculiar Triumph of Professor Branestawm*, and some of this many-sided genius's striking insights into the English language in *Professor Branestawm's Dictionary*. For readers of nine and over.

Professor Branestawm
up the Pole

NORMAN HUNTER

With illustrations by George Adamson

PUFFIN BOOKS
in association with The Bodley Head

Puffin Books, Penguin Books Ltd, Harmondsworth, Middlesex, England
Penguin Books Inc., 7110 Ambassador Road, Baltimore, Maryland 21207, U.S.A.
Penguin Books Australia Ltd, Ringwood, Victoria, Australia
Penguin Books Canada Ltd, 41 Steelcase Road West, Markham, Ontario, Canada
Penguin Books (N.Z.) Ltd, 182–190 Wairau Road, Auckland 10, New Zealand

—

First published by The Bodley Head 1972
Published in Puffin Books 1975

—

Copyright © Norman Hunter, 1972
Illustrations © The Bodley Head Ltd 1972

—

Made and printed in Great Britain by
Hazell Watson & Viney Ltd, Aylesbury, Bucks
Set in Monotype Baskerville

Professor Branestawm
would like to dedicate this book
to two special friends:
J. M. T. and Kaye Webb.

Contents

Professor Branestawm up the Pole

PROFESSOR BRANESTAWM had a new next-door neighbour, Commander Hardaport (Retired), a ferociously enthusiastic, yachting sort of Commander. He wore a white-topped yachting cap all day, and sometimes all night if he forgot to take it off. And in his garden he had a flagstaff on which he flew a most elegant flag.

He got up every morning at sunrise to hoist the flag up the pole and was always most particular to lower it again at sunset, because leaving flags out all night is highly irregular and very bad manners. It was awkward for Commander Hardaport sometimes in the winter, when he went to tea with friends, because, right in the middle of tea and intensive talk about spinnakers and yardarms, sunset would come on. Then he had to dash home to lower his flag, and by the time he got back his friends had finished the cakes (but not, of course, the yachting conversation, which, unlike flags, can quite properly go flying on all night).

'Flagstaff's looking a bit dirty,' he said to himself one morning. 'Most un-white flagstaff I've ever seen. This won't do at all. I'll have to get to action stations. But what course to set? Re-paint it? Then what? The flagstaff will get dirty again.' His naval mind revolved rapidly both forward and astern. 'What I need,' he said, 'is some flagstaff paint that won't get dirty. I know –

I'll get Professor Branestawm to invent some. Right. Ahoy there, Professor Branestawm!' he shouted over the fence.

Mrs Flittersnoop, the Professor's housekeeper, was in the middle of hanging out the washing. 'I'm afraid Professor Branestawm is out,' she said. She wasn't afraid of it really, but was actually glad because it gave her a chance to tidy the place up a bit. 'Can I give him a message when he comes back?'

'Thank you, but this is complicated,' said the Commander. 'I'd better send him a signal. Don't want to get things confused.' And he stumped into his house, and went into a tiny little room with a round porthole window and walls smothered in telescopes and charts and binnacles and bollards and hung about with warps and halliards.

'Dear Professor Branestawm,' he wrote, and was just going to ask the Professor to invent a never-get-dirty paint when an idea struck him amidships. After all, inventing a paint was rather a silly job for an inventing professor. The paint shop could do that. He had a much more important thing for Professor Branestawm to do.

He finished the letter, put it in an envelope, addressed it 'To Professor Branestawm. Message from the flagstaff' which was another of his seagoing jokes, and handed it over to Mrs Flittersnoop.

Then he wrote another letter to the paint shop saying, 'Will you please supply me with some white paint for my flagstaff. And I want paint that will never get dirty.' Then his pen, which had gone a bit scratchy, ran out of ink and he had to sign the note 'Hector Hardaport (Retired)' in pencil. But he used blue pencil to make it look as nautical as possible.

'Ah,' said Professor Branestawm, when he read the Commander's letter. 'A most interesting and unusual request.' He looked at the letter through each of his five pairs of spectacles and then through several pairs at once. 'The Commander wishes me to invent a flagstaff-painting machine,' he said.

'Well I never, sir,' said Mrs Flittersnoop. 'These naval gentlemen have some very strange ideas at times. Or perhaps I should say, rum ideas.' These seafaring jokes were catching.

Then the Professor went into his inventory to invent the flagstaff-painting machine.

'I could, of course, – ah – do it by first inventing a gatepost-painting machine and then re-inventing it much taller,' he said to himself. 'Or I might just invent a painting machine with a special adjustment for height and width. But then again I could invent a machine through which one pushed the – um – ah – flagstaff to paint it, but that might be awkward as the Commander would possibly not want to take the flag-staff down.'

After inventing like this for a while, the Professor finally got down to the flagstaff-painting machine, which was a device that you rode rather like a bicycle and it climbed up the flagstaff while you did the paint-ing.

Then he set off for Great Pagwell High Street, think-ing he might meet the Commander cruising about among the shops. And he hadn't got far when he met the Commander, rolling nautically down the High Street in a way that made you feel there was a heavy swell running, and that the High Street was taking it green over the bows. He was smoking a pipe that sent out such a smoke screen that the Professor wouldn't have seen him only he happened to be looking the other way. That caused him to run into the Commander, who bellowed, 'Hard astern both!', shook the Professor by the hand, and said, 'Fancy meeting you on a collision course, Professor! How's the machine coming on?'

'I – er – am glad to say it is all ready, Commander,' said the Professor. 'Where would you like it delivered?'

'On to the jolly old flagstaff!' cried the Commander, laughing like a ship's ventilator with the wind. 'I will go and arrange for you to carry out the operation.'

He gave the Professor a hearty seafaring clap on the back which shook all his spectacles off and, before the Professor had time to say anything, he was off in a cloud of heavy smoke.

The next day Professor Branestawm, accompanied by his flagstaff-painting machine, came over the fence. He was dressed in some painter's overalls lent to him by Mrs Flittersnoop's sister Aggie's cousin Bert. They were on the big side and Mrs Flittersnoop had fixed them up with plenty of safety pins.

He looked up at the flagstaff, which appeared to be at least two miles high. Then he clamped the painting machine round the bottom of the flagstaff and got into the saddle.

'Here's the paint,' said the Commander, giving him a tin with a handle on it. 'And a brush.'

'Er – ah – thank you,' said the Professor. He put the tin of paint into the paint-holder on the machine and put the brush in his mouth so as to have both hands free to start the machine, which was necessary as the machine had innumerable buttons and levers.

He pulled two levers and twiddled a wheel. With a series of grunts, squeaks and rattles the machine began very slowly to climb the flagstaff and the Professor began to paint.

Squeak rattle, zimzim, popetty clank, went the machine. *Slip, slop, slosh,* went the Professor with the paint brush.

'Avast there!' shouted the Commander. 'What are you starting at the bottom for?'

'Because one must always start at the bottom,' said the Professor. 'All the best copybooks say so. You could not have risen to become a Commander by starting at the top as an Admiral. There is also the ratio of height tolerance to speed to be considered. If, for instance,' he waved both hands and fell off the seat of the machine, 'if, for instance, you get into a motor-car and start driving at a hundred miles an hour right away you are liable to – um – ah – have an accident because you have not had time to accustom yourself to the speed.'

'Hrmmph. Quite,' said a voice from behind. It was the Professor's old friend, Colonel Dedshott of the Catapult Cavaliers, who had just arrived on his horse, which was rather given to starting off at full speed if it could.

'So,' said the Professor, climbing back on the seat of the painting machine, 'you start slowly and gradually build up the speed, and so become used to the fast movement by degrees.'

He was nine inches up the flagstaff when Mrs Flittersnoop from next door called out, 'Telephone, sir,' and the Professor had to go rushing in to answer the telephone. But it was only the Vicar to ask how the flagstaff painting was going.

Next time the Professor was two feet nine inches up

the flagstaff when Mrs Flittersnoop called out that lemonade and sponge cakes were ready. So they all knocked off for a lemonade break which is the same as a coffee break but sometimes takes longer. It certainly did this time because no sooner had Commander Hardaport finished a stirring yarn about naval escapades than Colonel Dedshott, not to be outdone by a mere sailor, opened fire with an intrepid story about fighting against dreadful odds in the desert. And that reminded the Professor of the time he invented an outrageous cactus that put umbrellas up if you watered it.

So, after all that, the lemonade break lasted until lunchtime. Mrs Flittersnoop said she had just made one of her special steak and kidney puddings, and had new potatoes and peas to go with it, and a frightfully fancy trifle to follow it. Neither the military nor the naval part of the party could resist that, and even the Professor actually ate lunch because his mind wasn't entirely on the flagstaff-painting project.

And they all ate so much they went to sleep afterwards and woke up only just in time for tea. Then the Vicar called to see how they were getting on and the Headmaster of Pagwell College came round with advice about flagstaffs, which he felt competent to give as he had once had to climb the college flagstaff to get down his mortarboard hat, which an energetic pupil had put up there for a joke.

By the time they had got through all these serious matters it was too dark to do any painting, so the company dismissed until next day.

Next day it rained, and apart from a suggestion from the Professor that they should bring the flagstaff indoors to paint it, which was ruled out as nobody had a room long enough, the entire day was wasted.

But at last there came a day when it was fine, and the Commander and the Colonel had run out of thrilling stories, and Mrs Flittersnoop had gone to the supermarket and couldn't serve lemonade and sponge cakes and the Vicar and the Headmaster were too busy to call, and flagstaff painting could therefore begin in earnest.

Slap, slosh, slap, the Professor painted away at the flagstaff. *Creak, creak, rattle, squeak*, the machine gradually crawled up the staff as he painted. People stopped outside to offer useful advice and make encouraging

noises. Up and up went the Professor until at last he was right at the top and the whole flagstaff was gleaming white. Certain portions of the Colonel and the Commander were also gleaming white where the Professor had spilt a drop or two of paint now and again.

But oh good gracious! Of course the Professor ought to have realized that the higher up he painted the flagstaff the more he wouldn't be able to get down because of the wet paint. But he had been so taken up with arguing with the Colonel and the Commander about the right way to paint the flagstaff that he had never thought about the paint being wet.

But oh good gracious ninety times over, there was something else! Something the Professor couldn't have remembered because he didn't know about it. And neither did the Commander.

When the Commander had written the letter to the paint shop asking for paint that would never get dirty, his pen had gone scratchy at the end and run out of ink and he had had to sign it in pencil. But the Commander hadn't noticed that the running-out pen had written the word 'dirty' so that it looked like 'dry' because some of the letters hadn't come out. So the Commander's letter had asked the paint shop for paint that would never get dry. And the paint shop people hadn't worried. They had just put a bit more linseed oil, or whatever it is, into the paint and sent it off.

So there it was, and there was Professor Branestawm, stuck on top of a lovely, clean, newly-painted, sixty-foot flagstaff which would never dry to let him come down.

Colonel Dedshott and the Commander had no idea things were as awful as they really were. But Professor Branestawm had. He had just remembered to read the instructions on the tin of paint now the job was finished, because that is when people usually read instructions if they ever do.

'Dedshott!' he called through his portable radio, that fortunately he had taken up with him in case he wanted to listen to any learned talks while he painted. And fortunately again, it was a radio for broadcasting from as well as listening to. 'Dedshott!' he said. 'I have just seen printed on this tin of paint that it will never get dry. I am stuck up here for ever. Get help!'

The Colonel and the Commander couldn't hear him. They hadn't got any radio receivers. But the Professor's radio went right into the Pagwell Broadcasting Company's programme. Mrs Flittersnoop, listening in the kitchen to Willie Wibblesome's half-hour, heard the Professor's call for help right in the middle of a song about someone loving someone for three times over.

'Lawks a mussy me!' she cried. 'If that isn't the Professor calling for help.' She dashed out into the garden and shouted to Commander Hardaport, 'It's the Professor, sir! Broadcasting on the wireless, sir! Asking for Colonel Dedshott to help, sir. Something about the paint never drying, he said.'

Commander Hardaport dashed into his house and came out again with a loud hailer of the kind that ships use to argue with one another at sea.

Then there started a most unlikely, complicated, long distance conversation, with the Commander and Colonel Dedshott loudhailing questions up to the Professor, and the Professor answering them through Mrs Flittersnoop's kitchen radio. And Mrs Flittersnoop running backwards and forwards with messages.

'By Jove, what!' cried the Colonel, his head spinning

round and round faster than it did when he was listening to one of the Professor's complicated explanations. 'How are we to get him down, Commander? No equipment for climbing wet flagstaffs. Never found an enemy up a flagstaff yet. You get the Navy, sir. They're used to climbing masts and things. They'll have the Professor down in no time, by gad!'

'Nothing of the kind!' protested Commander Hardaport. 'Not even the Navy can climb masts covered in wet paint. Ridiculous, sir. Fetch the Fire Brigade!'

'Right! Good idea!' shouted the Colonel.

He burst off and almost immediately Commander Hardaport was hit with a clever idea. If the Navy couldn't climb wet flagstaffs they *could* erect dry flagstaffs. Yes, yes, indeed. And he, Commander Hardaport, would get them to erect one next to his, so that they could get the Professor down.

'Can't hold on much longer!' came an anguished message from the Professor, via Mrs Flittersnoop.

'Hold on just a bit,' shouted the Commander through his loud hailer. He dashed into the Professor's house and got Mrs Flittersnoop to help him out with an armchair. Then tying this to a rope with many nautical knots, he threw the rope up to the Professor, so that he didn't have to go on sitting in the painting machine, which was hard and irksome for sitting in for ever.

After that things happened fast and thick.

The Professor hauled up the armchair by the rope and fixed it on top of the flagstaff, and sent the rope down for a little table and some books to read. Then he got the Commander to hoist up some of his inventing tools and before long he was sitting up on the flagstaff, sixty feet above everything, inventing like mad.

'Now if I could – ah – um – invent a way of getting down from here . . .' he said. But that was the one thing he couldn't do.

Meantime the Fire Brigade arrived and so did the Navy, or at least some of it. The flagstaff erecting began in earnest but didn't get on very fast because the firemen and their ladder kept getting tangled up with the sailors and their flagstaff.

'Avast there!' shouted the Commander. 'Lower away, haul up a bit! Keep that ladder away there!'

And the Fire Brigade chief was shouting to the firemen, and Colonel Dedshott was shouting to the Professor through the loud hailer. And the Professor was shouting back to the Colonel via Mrs Flittersnoop and the kitchen radio. And the road was thicker with sightseers than if it had been Lord Mayor's Show day.

Three times the Navy got their flagstaff up at the same time as the Fire Brigade got their ladder up. Firemen ran up the ladder and slid down the flagstaff, while sailors swarmed up the flagstaff and ran down the ladder. The Professor invented several kinds of paint that would dry as soon as you put them on, and one that came out in little steps so that you could go down them like a staircase.

But the ladder and flagstaff weren't near enough for the Professor to come down.

Colonel Dedshott began to see visions of himself going up the spare flagstaff on horseback to have tea with the Professor. Mrs Flittersnoop started wondering how she was going to haul meals up a flagstaff. The Mayor's wife, who was used to doing meals on wheels, offered to try her hand at meals on ropes. The Colonel and the Commander sent up a camp bed and some of Mrs Flittersnoop's second-best blankets.

Then along came the Pagwell Electricity Department with one of those tall tower arrangements they use for putting new lamps in the lamp-posts.

'Soon have you down from there, now, sir,' said the chief electricity man, winding the tower up alongside the Professor.

But by now Professor Branestawm was so comfortable on top of the flagstaff and found it so peaceful with nobody to disturb his inventing and no telephone calls and no bills able to reach him, that he wanted to stay up there.

The electricity chief, always willing to help, rigged up a nice street lamp so that the Professor could see after dark.

'But he can't stay up there for ever!' said Dr Mumpzanmeazle.

'Hrmmph!' said Colonel Dedshott.

'Ridiculous!' snorted Commander Hardaport (Retired).

'Oh dearie, dearie me!' wailed Mrs Flittersnoop.

'I fear this is most – – most – er – er,' said the Vicar.

And goodness knows what would have been the end of it all, but just then it came on to rain. It pelted. It poured. The looking-on crowds went home. The Fire Brigade went off in a hurry reckoning the rain could put out any fires that happened, and the Navy left because it was sunset and they had to haul their flags down.

But fortunately the electricity man and his tower stayed on because providing light, even in the rain, was his job. And the Professor, who wouldn't have come down to save getting himself wet because he could have had an umbrella slung up to him, was absolutely terrified that his books and inventing tools would be spoiled.

So he crawled gingerly on to the electric light tower and was lowered gently to the ground amid three cheers, one from Colonel Dedshott, one from Commander Hardaport and a very faint but none the less enthusiastic one from Mrs Flittersnoop.

But the non-drying paint on the flagstaff collected all the dirt it could find, and it looked more of an unnautical mess than ever. And worst of all the Commander couldn't hoist his flag up it or the flag would have got covered in paint, which would have been frightful.

But everything ended up very nicely after all. The Commander took down the dirty flagstaff and instead Professor Branestawm invented a special automatic, self-acting flagstaff that hoisted the flag all by itself at sunrise and lowered it again at sunset. So the Commander didn't have to get up at the crack of dawn any more, and neither did he have to come dashing back from enjoyable parties to haul the flag down.

And the Branestawm automatic flagstaff not only hoisted the flag every day at sunrise, including Sundays and holidays, but it also played *God Save the Queen* as it did so. It played it fairly quietly, of course, so as not to disturb the neighbours, which was important, particularly as Professor Branestawm was one of the neighbours.

But Commander Hardaport (Retired) still felt he ought to wake up at sunrise anyway, so as to stand up and salute while the flag went up and the music went off.

There's no satisfying some people.

2

The Secret Machine

PROFESSOR BRANESTAWM, of course, was well known for being so taken up with thinking about extraordinary things that he hardly ever had time to think about ordinary things. If he hadn't been, this story would never have happened. But there you are. Simple things never occurred to the Professor.

Mrs Flittersnoop tapped politely on the door of Professor Branestawm's study. Then she flung it open.

'A gentleman to see you, sir,' she said.

'Professor Branestawm?' said the gentleman. 'My name is Twidley. I believe you invent things.'

'Er – yes,' said the Professor wondering if Mr Twidley invented his name.

'I have an idea,' went on Mr Twidley, sitting down and moving his chair forward so that it immediately became very unsteady owing to one leg, which was shorter than the others, getting moved off the book it was propped up on. 'I have an idea for a machine that I want you to invent for me,' he went on. 'If it is successful it will make us both rich for the rest of our lives. Think of that! And when I say rich, my dear Professor, I don't mean just merely rich enough to buy a few motor-cars every week and have a different suit for every day of the year. I mean so rich that you can never possibly spend all your money however hard you try. Wealthy enough to own the universe . . .'

'Ah – um – er,' said the Professor. He didn't much like the look of Mr Twidley.

Mr Twidley was fat. Not jolly and round and fat, but just fat fat. He had podgy hands. His face was so smooth it looked as if he had it specially ironed every day. His eyes were little, and he kept licking his lips.

'Well, what do you say, Professor?' he asked. 'Are you willing to invent my machine and be rich for life? Ha ha!' He laughed like a man who has been told a joke he doesn't see.

'Um – well – I must know something about it before I can – er – give an – um – ah opinion,' said the Professor. 'If it is any sort of machine for blowing people up so as to get their money, I am afraid I must decline to consider it. We scientific people have to be most careful, you know. Most careful.' He pushed some papers aside and upset the ink.

'Of course, of course. Why, my dear Professor, I know how careful you have to be. Believe me, I do,' said Mr Twidley, helping to mop up the ink with the Professor's handkerchief. 'My idea is nothing so terrible as you suggest. Listen . . .' He edged his chair nearer to the Professor, where the short chair leg wedged itself on another book and made things steady again. He whispered rapidly, and the Professor's eyes opened so wide, as he listened, that his spectacles didn't fit. 'Simple. We can be the richest men in the world.' He licked his lips again and laughed like a man who has seen a joke he hasn't been told.

'Um – most interesting, I must say,' said the Professor. 'I had never thought of that. It certainly sounds excellent to me. And there should not be many difficulties.' He began one of his long explanations, but Mr Twidley licked his lips and stopped him.

'Pardon me, Professor. I leave the details to you, of course. Make a machine for me, and one for youself. In return for making mine you can have yours. That will be better than any sum of money I could pay you, as you will appreciate. But . . .' He licked his lips again, and his little eyes sparkled. 'There must be absolute secrecy, Professor. Nobody must know of this. I'm sure that a man of your experience and qualifications will understand that,' he purred.

'Yes, yes, of course, naturally,' said the Professor. 'I will start inventing the machine at once.'

'Excellent, excellent, my dear sir,' said Mr Twidley. 'I will call again – shall we say in a week's time? Yes, a week's time. I wish you all success. Goodbye, Professor. Goodbye.' And he was gone, laughing to himself like a man who has seen a joke he doesn't intend to tell anyone else.

A few days later Colonel Dedshott called to see the Professor, but saw Mrs Flittersnoop instead.

'The Professor's in his inventory, sir,' said Mrs Flittersnoop. 'And he's come over that strange lately I don't know what to make of it, sir, that I don't.'

'Ha!' said Colonel Dedshott, who knew pretty well how strange the Professor usually was and wondered how he could come over more so. 'Busy, I suppose? Inventing things. Clever, ha! I'll go round and see him.'

'I'm sure, I hope you will, sir,' said Mrs Flittersnoop. 'But he's been getting very tiresome to deal with, I must say. The trouble I've had getting him to take his meals you wouldn't believe. Still, it's all in the day's work as you might say, and I never was a one to complain.'

Colonel Dedshott rapped briskly on the door of the Professor's inventory.

'How many times am I to tell you I don't want any dinner? Do please go away, Mrs Flittersnoop,' came the Professor's voice from inside, followed by a shattering noise.

'All right, it's only me, Dedshott,' said the Colonel. He opened the door and stepped inside the inventory. Instantly the Professor swung round from his work and hurriedly flung a blanket over his invention. But it was a large blanket and got itself flung over the Colonel and part of the Professor as well.

'Aah – my dear Dedshott,' gasped the Professor, coming out from under a fold of blanket and getting his invention all bundled up in the rest of it. 'I am afraid you have arrived at a rather inopportune time. I am engaged upon a very confidential invention. The secret would surprise you if I were permitted to reveal it.'

'Ha!' said the Colonel, counting his medals to see that none of them had got tangled up in the blanket. 'What's it this time? Machine for inventing inventions?'

'No,' said the Professor, 'although I have some interesting notes on just such an idea as that. No, no, I cannot discuss this matter. It is most secret. Please go away.'

'Tut, tut,' snorted the Colonel. He had never known the Professor like this before. Usually he was all too eager to explain his inventions and make the Colonel's head go round and round with the complicated details.

'But –' he began.

'No, no, please, dear me, you make it most difficult for me, Dedshott. Go away, there's a good fellow. Come and see me in, let me see, oh yes, in a week's time, and I shall have a really remarkable surprise for you.' And the Colonel had to be content with that.

And Mrs Flittersnoop had to be content to have no end of bother with the Professor's meals.

Exactly a week later, Mr Twidley called to see if his machine was ready. And strangely enough it was.

'Really, my dear Professor, I must congratulate you,' purred Mr Twidley, licking his lips and sitting on the edge of a chair, while the Professor worked the machine for him. 'Now that is most ingenious, *most* ingenious.'

'Er – um – yes, of course,' muttered the Professor. 'But science, you know, Mr Twidley. We Professors

have to know a great number of things, so that it is not
so – um – surprising as you might think.'

'Quite, quite,' said Mr Twidley. He licked his lips
five times, wrapped the highly successful machine very
neatly in brown paper and, after long drawn out polite-
nesses on both sides, went off with his parcel. And as
he went he laughed like a man who has seen all the
jokes that haven't yet been made.

'Ah,' said the Professor, rubbing his hands. He went
to his inventory and brought out the second machine
which he had made for himself when he made the other
one for Mr Twidley. It worked just as well. In fact, it
worked rather better, because being the second one he
had made, he had got himself rather used to making
it.

'A most gratifying piece of work, I must say,' murmured the Professor.

Then the door opened, and in came Colonel Dedshott, and, as the Professor had no blankets to hide the
machine with, he tried to cover it with a rug the Colonel
was standing on and push it up the chimney before it
was noticed.

'Another secret invention, what?' said the Colonel.
'All right, Branestawm, I won't look. No business of
mine.'

The Professor hesitated. He always explained his
inventions to the Colonel, and somehow he felt he
wasn't getting so much pleasure out of his machine as
he might be, through having to keep it a secret from
him. Still, keeping a thing a secret when it was all
successfully finished was different. Would there be any
harm in showing the Colonel what it did so long as he
didn't explain how it managed to do it? Surely not.

Colonels could be discreet. The Army understood secret things.

'All right, now what?' asked the Colonel, who had been hiding his eyes in a corner while the Professor hid the machine somewhere else, and was getting rather tired of watching a blue tulip with two stalks that happened to be on the wallpaper in front of him.

'Well – er – Dedshott,' said the Professor cautiously. 'I think perhaps it might be permissible for me to demonstrate my new success to you, provided, Dedshott, you will agree to say nothing about it. Confidential, you understand?'

'Quite, secret, not a word, what! Rely on me!' said the Colonel, rapidly coming away from the blue tulip.

The Professor demonstrated his invention. He forgot to be as cautious as he had intended and explained it all as well, but it didn't matter, because the Colonel's head went round and round as usual, and he didn't understand nine-tenths of it. But what he did understand was quite enough.

'Good gracious, Branestawm!' he cried. 'You can't do that! My word, good job you told me! They'll put you in prison!'

'Eh?' said the Professor.

His secret and confidential invention was a machine for making money! Yes, it was. You made up your mind whether you wanted fifty pence pieces or pound notes or what. You put a real one into its proper slot, as a copy for the machine. You turned a handle, and out came as many fifty pence pieces or pound notes as you liked. Most astounding. But also most drastically illegal.

Of course, anybody but Professor Branestawm would

have thought about that the very second Mr Twidley said what his idea was. But the Professor never got as far as even wondering whether you were allowed to invent money-making machines. He was too taken up and excited about another chance to invent an astonishing and world-shaking invention to think about such uninteresting things as whether you were allowed to do it.

'Don't you know you aren't allowed to make money like that?' gasped the Colonel. 'Nobody is allowed to make money except the Mint. Good job you told me about this, Branestawm. Just in time to stop you, what? By Jove, you know, you are a one! If you went making your own money, you'd be in prison.'

'Dear me, is that so?' said the Professor. 'Really, Dedshott, I fear that is a point of view which I had overlooked. That makes things most awkward. Mr Twidley will be very disappointed.' Suddenly the Professor jumped to his feet. 'Oh my goodness, Dedshott, we must find him at once! Yes, yes, at once. He instructed me to make the machines, you know. He took one away. He will be making money, and they will put him in prison.'

'Pah!' snorted the Colonel. 'Serve him right! Twidley, did you say? The twister! The scoundrel! He must have known very well this is not allowed. He'll be making money in secret with your machine, Branestawm. I hope they catch him. Better smash this one now.'

'Yes, yes!' said the Professor. They grabbed pokers and attacked the machine. Three times the Professor hit the Colonel by mistake, but luckily only hit him on a medal, which was noisy, but didn't hurt. Twice the

Colonel missed the machine with the poker and fell on it, which smashed it even better.

At last it was reduced ro ruins.

'Now you're safe, Branestawm!' said the Colonel. 'If Twidley is caught, nobody will know you made the machine.'

'Er – um –' said the Professor, 'I'm afraid we cannot be so sure about that, Dedshott. I rather believe I used an old brass plate with my name on it as part of the machine. Tut, tut, most awkward, I had no idea these difficulties would arise.'

But Colonel Dedshott wasn't waiting to have ideas about anything. He grabbed the Professor by the hand, and rushed him off to find Mr Twidley and smash his machine too.

Alas, the Professor either never had Mr Twidley's address, or else he had forgotten it. They asked at all the railway stations, they looked up telephone directories, they asked bus conductors, errand boys and postmen, but none of them could help.

'If only we dared ask a policeman,' groaned the Professor, who always asked policemen when he couldn't find his way home, which was rather often.

They went wearily back to the Professor's house.

And there stood two policemen on the doorstep!

'Come to arrest you, Branestawm!' breathed the Colonel. 'Quick, we must use strategy!'

He dragged the Professor through some very prickly bushes and got him somehow up a drain-pipe into his bedroom.

'Don't go out or show yourself,' commanded the Colonel. 'I'll find that Twidley at once, if it takes me a year!' And off he shot, down the drain-pipe and away,

while the Professor, who didn't think he cared much
about the Colonel's strategy, crawled under the bed
with a book about butterflies.

The policemen went away from the front door and
tried the back door. Mrs Flittersnoop came back from
some shopping and ran into them. Thank goodness she
didn't know where the Professor was! A lot of talking
and waving of hands went on, and presently the policemen went inside with Mrs Flittersnoop.

Colonel Dedshott was still hunting frantically for Mr
Twidley, Professor Branestawm was still hiding under
the bed and Mrs Flittersnoop had already opened the
door to the policemen, when who should walk in but
Mr Twidley himself!

'Professor Branestawm!' he shouted. Then he caught
sight of a policeman's helmet on a chair in the hall, and
he began silently and craftily to creep out again. He
slithered to the door. He eased it open a crack. He
peered round. Then he sat down with a bump on the
mat, for Colonel Dedshott had burst in through the
door all frantic at not being able to find him.

'Branestawm,' he called. Then, 'My word, *there* you
are! Got you, by Jove!'

He grabbed Mr Twidley, and Mr Twidley grabbed
him.

'I want Professor Branestawm!' cried Mr Twidley.
'The machine he invented for me doesn't work. It is of
no use. It must be altered.'

'Hey?' gasped the Colonel.

'Dear me!' said the Professor, forgetting everything
and rushing downstairs. 'I cannot understand that at
all, Mr Twidley. Dear, dear! The other machine was

quite satisfactory. Perhaps I had become rather more used to it by then. But all the same . . .'

'It is no use!' snarled Mr Twidley. 'It does not make money. It only turns out the money I put in for it to copy. You're a fraud, sir, that's what you are. I've a good mind to call in the police.'

'Now then, what's all this here?' said a gruff voice. And the two policemen came out of the kitchen to see who was talking about them.

There was a cloud of dust and a bang, as Mr Twidley shot rapidly out of the front door, up the path, over the gate and away.

'What was the gentleman doing?' enquired the policemen.

'He – er – ah – hum – yes,' said the Colonel, suddenly realizing he had better not say much about Mr Twidley in case it got the Professor into trouble for making the money machine. 'Er, that is to say, constable, he was a client of the Professor's.'

The two policemen looked at each other and were just beginning to wonder what was what, when Mrs Flittersnoop put her head round the door and said, 'Tea's ready, boys.'

And, as tea was what the policemen had come for, and not for the Professor, they said, 'That'll be all right then, sir. Good day to you.' They put on their helmets, marched out of the front door, round to the back, and into the kitchen for the tea, while Colonel Dedshott and Professor Branestawm collapsed into a chair each, and felt glad things were over at last. And even the Professor for once felt secretly relieved that a machine of his had failed to work properly.

3

Mrs Flittersnoop Makes some Cakes

MRS FLITTERSNOOP was in several dithers. She didn't know what to do about things, she was sure.

'I'll never do it!' she said to herself. 'There just isn't the time. But there, I've promised and I can't let them down. Oh dearie, dearie me!'

'If it's about those grey socks of mine that need darning,' said Professor Branestawm, who had just come in, 'I can – um – ah – go out and buy some more.'

'Oh no, indeed sir,' said Mrs Flittersnoop, 'it's not the socks at all. It's the cakes for the Vicarage Garden Party.'

'But surely cakes do not need darning,' said the Professor, beginning to think that if they did, how inconvenient it was going to be, sewing up all those holes in crumpets, darning doughnuts and patching up pikelets.

'I shall never be able to get them done in time,' said Mrs Flittersnoop, taking no notice of what the Professor said. 'I had no idea when I promised to do them,' she went on, 'that they'd want so many. Twelve dozen jam tarts, indeed,' she said, spreading out her hands in a sort of twelve dozen way. 'And fourteen Swiss rolls, for goodness sake! Not to mention five dozen assorted meringues, six dozen doughnuts with jam and three dozen with holes, and eighty-five cup cakes and . . .'

'Well,' said the Professor, going all helpful and practical, 'if you haven't time to make them all we should just go out and buy them. If I can buy socks to save you darning them, why can't we buy cakes to save you making them?'

Mrs Flittersnoop gave a gasp and looked as if she had been struck by lightning.

'*Buy them*, did you say, sir?' She came over all dizzy, the walls shook a bit and three pictures went crooked.

Of course the Professor didn't know that going out and buying cakes is just never done. It isn't on. People aren't supposed to do it. Because if you go buying cakes and visitors say, 'Did you make them?' you've had it. You have to admit that you bought them and then leave the country quietly to avoid the scandal. Buy the cakes indeed! Oh dear no, Mrs Flittersnoop could never agree to such an antisocial, frightful, underhand, disgraceful kind of thing as that.

'Perhaps they could put off the Garden Party?' suggested the Professor.

But putting off Vicarage Garden Parties was only slightly less criminal than buying the cakes for them, so that was no good.

'Then tell them you can't do it,' said the Professor, getting a bit impatient because he had an invention simmering in his head and wanted to get on with it before it blew his spectacles off.

'Oh, I can't do *that*, sir!' said Mrs Flittersnoop. 'I promised. I can't let them down.'

'Well,' said the Professor, his brains beginning to whiz, 'there must be some way out of the difficulty. If a fisherman fails to catch any fish he can get away with it by buying some on the way home. All he has to do is tell the fishmonger to throw them to him so that he can say quite truthfully that he caught them. But one can hardly do that with cakes, can one? One doesn't catch cakes. Now I wonder,' he said to himself, 'if one could invent a means of buying cakes in such a manner as to be able to say truthfully that one made them. One could say,' he went on to himself, 'I really need ten dozen cakes but I can make do with nine dozen. Then if people asked if you made them you would say you made do.' It sounded all right, but the Professor couldn't see Mrs Flittersnoop doing it.

Then suddenly he saw daylight through the doughnuts and the Swiss rolls. A great gleam of hope shone past the meringues. Inspiration shouldered the jam tarts out of the way.

'Mrs Flittersnoop!' he cried. 'Mrs Flittersnoop, I have it! You *can* make the cakes in time, easily.'

Mrs Flittersnoop had been working out that she could almost do half the cakes in time by staying up all night, not having any meals, leaving the beds unmade, neglecting the ironing and getting the Professor to stay with Colonel Dedshott, out of the way.

'Yes, sir?' she said, feeling tired already.

'I shall invent a cake-making machine!' shouted the Professor. 'Why didn't I think of that before? You'll be able to make enough cakes for fifteen Vicarage Garden Parties in next to no time, by just pressing switches and pulling levers.'

'But I shan't be making them!' cried Mrs Flittersnoop. 'The machine will be doing it.'

'Tut tut!' said the Professor. 'That doesn't matter. When you make cakes by hand the oven does the cooking but that doesn't worry you. And you don't feel you haven't made a dress just because you put the material through a sewing machine. So you needn't feel you haven't made the cakes just because you've made them with my machine.'

'Yes indeed – I mean – no, I'm sure, sir,' said Mrs Flittersnoop, 'so I suppose.'

'Right,' said the Professor, getting all brisk and practical, 'you go and get the flour and currants and jam and things while I get the machine invented.' He shot out into his inventory, cleared a space on his bench and, with a cookery book in one hand, a spanner in the other and a wooden spoon behind his ear, he started inventing.

The Professor's automatic, self-propelled, electronically controlled, double reciprocating, sprocket-geared cake-making machine stood in the kitchen. The Professor stood on one side of it, and Mrs Flittersnoop stood the other side, which used up all the standing room.

'Now,' said the Professor, adjusting his spectacles and making explaining movements with his hands. 'Here are the buttons you press according to what sort of cakes you want. There is one for buns and one for tarts and one for doughnuts and so on. And underneath each button is a dial which you set to the number of each particular cake you require. Is that clear?'

'Oh yes indeed, I'm sure,' said Mrs Flittersnoop.

'Then,' said the Professor, 'having pressed the buttons and set the dials you simply pull this lever marked "Production Start" and the cakes will begin to come out here,' he pointed to a row of scoops. 'You will, of course,' he went on, 'take the precaution of placing a receptacle to receive the cakes.'

'Yes indeed, I'm sure, sir,' said Mrs Flittersnoop, reckoning that would be a wise precaution as she didn't want doughnuts and jam tarts all over the floor.

'There are one or two other – er – refinements,' added the Professor, coming round to the side of the machine and getting his coat pocket caught on the rotary tin opener, which opened his pocket rather more than it needed. 'For instance, Swiss roll will come out in one long length and you simply adjust this scale so that the machine will cut it into whatever lengths you require. You can thus have standard length, super long, family size, giant size or double tremendous, as you prefer. Or on the other hand you can have the Swiss roll in slices, thin, medium or thick.'

He moved round to the other side of the machine without any noticeable mishaps and went on.

'Here is the icing putter-on, with switches for different coloured icing and, in case you should require it, an almond paste layerer. The Swiss roll rollers are also coupled to the Chelsea bun twirlers to economize in mechanism and the jam tart fillers work in much the same way as the icing putter-on only rather different.'

'Yes indeed, I'm sure, sir,' gasped Mrs Flittersnoop, who couldn't think of anything else to say and was beginning to wish the Vicarage wouldn't have Garden Parties or else would have cakeless ones.

'Now,' said the Professor, 'just try your hand with the machine to make sure you understand it.'

Mrs Flittersnoop approached the machine with one hand held out, rather as she might have approached a large and overbearing horse with a lump of sugar.

'I think we'll try some jam doughnuts,' she said,

resisting the temptation to say 'Good dog' to the machine.

She pressed the doughnut button, dialled 6 and pulled the Production Start lever.

Whiz-z-z-z-z pop splutter, zoom zoom thud! The machine made assorted noises, emitted a smell of bakeries, gave out a good deal of heat and then, *plonk, plonk*, six times, six lovely round doughnuts rolled out of the scoop and under the table, as Mrs Flittersnoop in

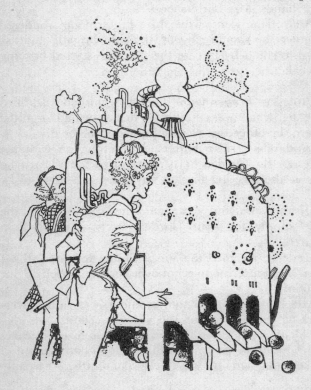

the excitement of the moment had forgotten to put a basket to catch them.

'Ah, most – er – satisfactory,' said the Professor, when they had gathered up all the doughnuts. 'Well, I'm sure you will be able to manage very well.' He put on a pudding basin in mistake for his hat but took it off again as it felt a bit hard. 'I'm going out for the rest of the day as I have – er – meetings to attend. I think I can safely leave the – um – ah – operation of the machine in your hands, Mrs Flittersnoop.'

And off he went, while Mrs Flittersnoop wondered whether she should ring up the Fire Brigade and ask them to stand by in case the machine started burning the cakes.

Professor Branestawm had just finished his third meeting, which was actually his first as he had forgotten where the other two were supposed to be held.

'And how is Mrs Flittersnoop getting on with the cakes for the Garden Party?' enquired the Vicar, who was at the meeting in case any prayers needed to be said.

'I can assure you, Vicar,' said the Professor, 'that the cake supply for your Garden Party is more than assured.'

'Indeed,' beamed the Vicar, 'I am delighted. But I hope Mrs Flittersnoop is not overworking herself on our account.'

Mrs Flittersnoop, at that moment, was rather over-working the machine on the Vicar's account.

Machinery noises filled the kitchen and so did cakes and buns of all kinds. Mrs Flittersnoop had run out of baskets long ago and was filling coal scuttles – carefully washed out first – with buns, and shoe boxes with meringues, and pails with cup cakes. Swiss rolls of assorted lengths were stacked shoulder high. Jam tarts were legion. The kitchen smelt like ten bakeries working overtime. It was as hot as a summer day and everything was confectionarily lovely.

'Well, I think that's really enough now,' said Mrs Flittersnoop. 'I'll stop the machine and get the cakes ready to take round to the Vicarage.'

But oh dear! The Professor had forgotten to show her how to turn the machine off. She tried to push the Production Start lever back but it wouldn't push. She tried to pick the cake buttons out but they stayed pushed in.

Jam tarts of all colours continued to emerge *rat-tat-tat-tat*, like a machine gun. Doughnuts went on rolling along like Old Man River.

'Oh dear a mussy me!' cried Mrs Flittersnoop. She waded through a sea of Swiss rolls and shook the machine. It responded with an increased flow of pink, white, green, yellow and pale blue meringues.

'Help!' she cried, as Chelsea buns came up to her waist.

She pushed at things, she pulled at things, she tried to twiddle things that were untwiddleable. And all the time the machine whizzed and hummed and surged out more and more assorted cakes quicker and quicker. The smell was delicious. The heat was overpowering. The kitchen would have been neck deep in cakes but fortunately the window was open and some escaped into the garden.

Mrs Flittersnoop struggled out of the kitchen to telephone the Fire Brigade.

Alas! A fire had broken out at the fire station, and the Fire Brigade was too busy to come.

A Swiss roll ten yards long coiled itself round Mrs Flittersnoop's legs like an enormous sponge snake.

'Help!' she gasped and tried to telephone Colonel Dedshott. But, oh drastic development, he was at that moment having tea and Swiss roll with General Shatterfortz!

Custard tarts, Banbury cakes and chunks of Battenberg cake with double thick almond icing were infiltrating the dining-room.

Mrs Flittersnoop dialled the Vicarage number but everybody was out at a service.

Mrs Flittersnoop kicked the Swiss roll away and rushed into the sitting-room, letting in a regiment of eclairs. She flung open the window and yelled for help amid cascades of cakes. And, good gracious, who should be going by but Colonel Dedshott, accompanied by two Catapult Cavaliers, on his way back from tea at the General's!

'By Jove, to the rescue, what!' roared the Colonel. 'Come on!' He dashed up to the front door, but Mrs Flittersnoop couldn't open it for him because she was beating off Banbury cakes. He charged round to the open window. A broadside of doughnuts came rolling at him. The Catapult Cavaliers trod on them and fell over, and their mouths were instantly filled with macaroons. Colonel Dedshott received a row of jam tarts on his chest, which covered his medals and made him look like a double set of traffic lights.

'Help!' gasped Mrs Flittersnoop.

The Colonel clambered in through the window and was engulfed in Chelsea buns.

And goodness knows what would have happened next if Professor Branestawm hadn't arrived! He was earlier than expected because he had arrived at the first meeting after the third meeting and found it was all over. He opened the door with his key and was immediately enveloped in mad cakery.

'Um, I fear Mrs Flittersnoop has rather overdone things,' he muttered. He pushed his way through to the kitchen and switched the machine off.

Clearing up all the cakes took a bit of time, but Colonel Dedshott sent for more Catapult Cavaliers and the Vicar obliged with some Boy Scouts. And between them they got all the cakes round to the Vicarage in good time for the Garden Party. And it was a record success, because owing to the prodigious amount of cakes, the Party ran for five days.

'Of course,' said Professor Branestawm, 'my machine did not go wrong. On the contrary, it went exceedingly right. It only needed switching off.'

Then Ye Olde Bun Shoppe of Great Pagwell, which had heard of the cake machine, bought it from the Professor, and Mrs Flittersnoop went on to a strict diet of bloater paste sandwiches, because she simply could not look a cake in the face again for ages.

4

A Brush with the Artists

A LARGE SQUARE ENVELOPE rested on the Professor's breakfast plate. He put it into the toast rack and tried to open a piece of toast with his knife, but Mrs Flitter-snoop came to the rescue and extracted from the envelope a large square card with wriggly gilt edges and very superior printing made to look as if it were writing.

'The Management of the Royal Pagwell Society of Arts requests the pleasure of the company of' and then, in rather squiggly writing, 'Professor Branestawm and friend' followed by 'at an exhibition of the work of Paul Palette-Brushleigh, Esq. R.P.S.A., to be opened by The Right Honourable Lord Pagwell of Pagwell at 3 p.m. on March 10.' Then it added in very small type, as if it hoped you wouldn't be able to read it, 'Tea will be served.'

'Ah – um – pictures,' said the Professor. 'Most interesting, I have no doubt. What friend can I take? Colonel Dedshott, I fear, would not appreciate pictures unless they were battle pictures and Dr Mumpzan-meazle seems to – ah – fancy only pictures of people's veins and muscles. Had it been an exhibition of stained glass windows I could have taken the Vicar, and no doubt Monsieur Bonmonjay of the Pagwell Hotel would have been interested if the pictures were still life, show-ing collections of food. But I believe Mr Palette-Brushleigh specializes in rather extraordinary paintings.

So I wonder who I could take. Yes, yes of course! Mrs Flittersnoop!' he called.

'Another egg, Professor?' asked Mrs Flittersnoop.

'Ah, ha ha, no,' said the Professor. 'My voice may have sounded a little cracked, but I was not laying an egg.'

'No indeed, I'm sure, sir,' said Mrs Flittersnoop, who began to see that this would be one of those days when the Professor was going to be jolly.

'You must – ah – come with me to this exhibition,' said the Professor, waving the card and making his tea go cold. 'You like pictures, I believe?' he added.

'Well yes sir, thanking you kindly,' said Mrs Flittersnoop, who *was* very fond of the pictures when they had exciting-looking gentlemen in them and plenty to cry about. But these weren't going to be moving pictures and she wasn't too sure if she would enjoy herself. But she was much too polite to say so and anyway she was rather honoured by being described as the Professor's *friend*.

The Grand Gallery of the Royal Pagwell Society of Arts was crowded. There were pictures, and there were people who had come to see them. There were arty-looking persons with beards, who were the ones who hung the pictures and swept the floors and cleaned the windows, and there were some severe-looking people with short hair and rimless eyeglasses and a very bank manager look, who were artists. There were tastefully arranged tea tables and there was Lord Pagwell, who although he wasn't a very large man, always seemed to give the impression that the room was full of him, and on these occasions he was certainly very full of himself.

But before he could start opening the exhibition the

Secretary of the Arts Society popped up and gave the audience what he called a brief history of the Society, which took a very long time. Then a big beard with someone behind it got up and said that Lord Pagwell needed no introduction, but took simply ages to introduce him. After that, Lord Pagwell, who had brought pages of notes for his speech, secretly tore them all up and said this was a time for pictures, not words, and he declared the exhibition open.

'Er – ah – hum,' said Professor Branestawm, looking at the pictures through various spectacles.

One picture was called 'Loneliness' and consisted of hundreds of coloured dots of different shapes. Another was 'Trees by a river' and showed two very upstanding lettuces and a cup of tea. There was one very narrow picture, five feet long and three inches high, painted purple all over with a black squiggle in one corner, and that was called 'Evening'.

'Er – ah – most interesting, but most puzzling and exceedingly not understandable,' murmured the Professor, looking rather nervously at a big picture of ferocious eyes clustered round a frying pan.

'Well, I never did, sir,' said Mrs Flittersnoop, caught between a picture of two bent lamp-posts in a bath and one of rows of empty bottles, all the wrong shape. 'They're not very good, are they? Indeed, I'm sure, sir, my little nephew could do better.'

'Pah!' snorted a voice behind them, and a very skinny, wild-looking little man with a lot of hair said, 'You betray your ignorance, madam. Your small middle class mind fails to appreciate the deeper meaning behind these pictures.'

'Ah!' said Professor Branestawm, who wasn't going

to have Mrs Flittersnoop spoken to like that. 'And who are you, pray, who can appreciate the inner meaning of this – er – um – ah – tarra-diddle of paint splashing?'

'I am Paul Palette-Brushleigh,' said the skinny little man, drawing himself up to his full height, which was nothing to speak of. 'You look an intelligent man. How can you tolerate such uninformed criticism from your companion?'

'I am Professor Branestawm,' said the Professor, taking all his spectacles off and staring at the skinny little man, who looked rather like one of his own pictures. 'And I – ah – agree entirely with this lady's comments.'

'Huh!' snorted Mr Palette-Brushleigh, shaking his hair about and making quite a draught. 'And I suppose you, like your companion's relative, could do better yourself?'

'Yes,' snapped the Professor. 'I not only can produce better pictures, but I *shall*. I shall invent a machine, my good sir,' he said, 'that will paint better pictures than you have ever dreamed of! And what is more,' he flung out his arms and knocked Mrs Flittersnoop's hat crooked, 'they will be pictures that look like something!'

Mr Palette-Brushleigh snorted. 'Look like something indeed!' But the Professor didn't hear him. He and Mrs Flittersnoop had gone to tea, which was one of those buffet kind of teas, where you helped yourself to as much as you could eat or as much as you could carry, whichever was the greater, and then looked round and found there was nowhere to sit.

'I have arranged,' said the Professor to Colonel Dedshott next day, after telling him about the exhibition, 'to invent a picture-painting machine and the Royal Pagwell Society of Arts has agreed to exhibit a selection of the pictures it will produce.'

'My word, jolly good!' said Colonel Dedshott, who reckoned that anyone who could paint a picture of anything that looked like something was mighty clever. 'That'll show 'em!'

'I am also –' went on the Professor, putting the Colonel's medals straight as some of them had jumped over wrong side to the front when the Colonel got a bit excited. 'I am also going to – ah – demonstrate my machine to the Society,' he said.

'Bravo!' said the Colonel, making a note to have some Catapult Cavaliers lurking about at the demonstration in case there was trouble.

'And I thought perhaps,' added the Professor, 'that you would be good enough to sit for your portrait when my machine is ready.'

'Ha yes, rather!' cried the Colonel, who was always good enough to have his picture done, whether it was by exotic artists or little black cameras. He had an enormous painting over his fireplace of an ancestor of his, Major Dedshott, painted against a background of fire, cannonballs and clashing swords which was supposed to represent the Major at Waterloo. But as a matter of fact, although he had been at the Battle of Waterloo, it was a long time before he became a Major, and he was only there to help clean the Duke of Wellington's Wellington Boots, which he did well out of cannonball range, nowhere near any clashing swords and with no fire except the one in the grate.

Professor Branestawm's Picture-Painting Machine was giving him more trouble than his inventions usually did when he was inventing them because, being an artistic machine, it was a bit temperamental. It insisted on trying to paint autumn trees on the Professor's shirt front because it couldn't bear to see anything white without wanting to paint on it. It put several ruined castles on the inventory walls, which wasn't necessary as previous inventions had already made them look ruined enough. And twice it painted miniatures of railway stations on the buns Mrs Flittersnoop brought for the Professor's elevenses.

But at last the Professor got it finished and reasonably tamed, and set it to work. And very soon the Professor and his machine were out and about in the Pagwells, immortalizing the landscape, the buildings and some of the people, in paint.

Then along went the pictures to the Royal Pagwell Society of Arts, in a van from the Pagwell Furnishing Company, supplied by the manager, Mr Chintsbitz, who had a huge beard and felt well disposed to artists. The picture-painting machine went separately, in Mrs Flittersnoop's cousin Bert's cart, covered up with plastic tarpaulins so as to be as secret as possible.

The great day of the Branestawm exhibition of mechanically painted pictures arrived, right on the correct day, and Lord Pagwell, who loved opening exhibitions, actually made a speech lasting several minutes, most of which was taken up by frightfully funny stories about nearly everything except pictures.

But at last the exhibition was prised open, and cries of delight went up from everybody except a group of very contemporary artists, led by Mr Palette-Brushleigh, who shrank most energetically from anything in a frame if you could see which way up it was supposed to hang.

Professor Branestawm's machine had certainly excelled itself. There was a lovely landscape of Pagwell Canal by moonlight and one of the Pagwell gasworks in a thunderstorm. There were beautiful pictures of trees and forest glades and country cottages that would have graced the most expensive box of chocolates anyone could wish for. There were five portraits of Colonel Dedshott which would have terrified any enemy who happened to be within eyeshot. There was a still life of one of Mrs Flittersnoop's rice puddings that looked much less still and ten times as lively as any respectable pudding could hope to. There were pictures to delight the heart, to please the eye, to soothe the savage breast and exalt the down-hearted.

The exhibition was an enormous success. All the pictures were sold, the portraits of Colonel Dedshott to Colonel Dedshott, the landscape to Farmer Plownough, who enjoyed looking at a field he didn't have to plough, and to people who always liked a nice bit of English countryside as long as the weather was fine, which it always was in these pictures. The Mayor bought a picture of Pagwell Town Hall painted almost life-size with him standing in the doorway apparently holding the whole thing up. The Vicar bought a rather sweet little one of Pagwell Church with a halo round it. Lord Pagwell, who owned the Pagwell Publishing Company, bought the Flittersnoop rice pudding to use as the cover of a cookery book. And a threatening picture of very spidery machinery was acquired by Pagwell College. Mr Stinckz-Bernagh, the science master, thought it would be useful for demonstrating the impossibility of having five right angles in a square.

'And now, ladies and gentlemen,' said Lord Pagwell, after banging on an empty turpentine tin the Society had supplied for the purpose to get attention, 'we shall now see a demonstration of Professor Branestawm's wonderful machine actually painting pictures.'

'Here is the machine itself,' said Professor Branestawm, whisking a cloth dramatically off, and producing the machine, which looked at the assembled company as if it didn't think much of any of them as oil paintings.

'First of all we have the picture size adjuster,' said the Professor, moving corner-shaped bits of frame in and out, 'as it would be most inconvenient to set the machine painting a six-foot landscape if one had only a two-foot canvas. Here we have the subject-choosing dials.' The Professor pointed to a row of knobs labelled *Landscape, Seascape, Interior, Still life* and *Portrait*. 'This device,' he explained, 'makes it unnecessary to go out to nature in order to paint landscapes if you do not wish to do so.'

'Ha!' exclaimed the Advanced Artists, who never went out to nature as they were scared stiff of cows in fields.

The Professor adjusted his spectacles, turned the machine round, and wheeled it forward a bit.

'Here we have the perspective corrector,' he explained.

'Boo!' cried the Advanced Artists, who didn't agree with perspective because it was too difficult to do.

'This is the colour harmony disciplinizer,' said the Professor, pointing to an oval wheel, 'to obviate any possibility of getting discordant clashes of objectionable colour.'

'Yah!' shouted the Advanced Artists, whose main idea was to get as many clashes of colour as possible just to show that they weren't bound by the inhibiting rules of commonplace art.

'And here are the colour racks, the brush holders and the form analyser,' the Professor went on.

'Bravo, what!' grunted Colonel Dedshott who didn't see why the Advanced Artists should be the only ones to make remarks.

'I shall now set the machine to paint a picture,' said the Professor, stuffing all his five pairs of spectacles into three pockets, turning knobs and pressing buttons on the machine. He put a large canvas into the picture holder and pulled a lever.

Ziz, poppety, splop, slosh, went the machine, landing a dab of Prussian Blue accurately in the middle of the forehead of the largest Advanced Artist who had advanced a bit too near for its liking.

After a few minutes the whizzing and popping stopped. The Professor and two picture-hanging assistants lifted the picture out of the machine and put it on an easel.

'Good gracious!' exclaimed Lord Pagwell.

'*Most* remarkable,' said the Vicar.

'Bravo!' cried Colonel Dedshott.

'Pah!' snorted the Advanced Artists.

The picture showed a landscape with trees of all kinds, three fields, one ploughed, one full of daisies and one full of assorted cows, a river with yachts, an old water mill, seven fancy cottages, two ruined castles, a pond with ducks, three bridges, a farm with horses and hens, two gardens full of flowers, a woodland glade, a seashore with liners in the distance, a church with two spires, and some distant mountains, all seen through a window with abstract curtains in front of which was a table with a bowl of fruit, some flowers in a copper jug and a portrait of Lord Pagwell.

It was the picture to end all pictures.

There was a tremendous buzzing of conversation and

uttering of excitable exclamations as everyone crowded
round the picture and Lord Pagwell had to hit the
empty turpentine tin five times to get silence for his
next announcement.

'For the benefit of those who were unable to come
today,' he said, 'Professor Branestawm has kindly
consented to do another demonstration here tomorrow
at the same time.'

That night, when the moon turned the Gallery of the
Royal Pagwell Society of Arts into a very picturesque
mixture of deep purple shadows and pale green moonlight, a number of murky figures crept in.

They were members of the Way Ahead and Right
Outside Group of Advanced Artists and they were bent
on mischief. They were also bent nearly double so as
not to be seen through the windows. They were going
to muck up the Professor's beautiful painting machine
because they didn't agree with being shown up and
done down by a lot of cogwheels.

'Hist!' they said, histing.

'Shush!' they said, shushing.

They histed and shushed their way round the
machine, loosening screws and inserting plastic span-
ners of very bad design into the works. Then they crept
out, still histing and shushing while the moon went on
shining, never mind what Advanced Artists had been
doing.

Next day the Professor arrived to find everybody
there waiting to see the demonstration, some of whom
hadn't seen it and just couldn't wait to see it now, and
some who had seen it the day before and didn't believe

it, and wanted to see it again and see if they didn't believe it again.

'I have been asked that the machine do a painting of Pagwell High Street,' said the Professor, taking the cover off.

He didn't notice anything wrong, because the Way Ahead and Right Outside Group of Advanced Artists had been very crafty in their machinations on the machine.

He put in a canvas, made adjustments and pulled a lever.

Squeeeeek, scraach! Bang! yelled the machine feeling something was wrong with it. *Slip, plop, splash*, red, green, pink and blue paint shot about. Several of the ladies received very unfashionable spotted dresses and one or two Advanced Artists looked as if they had Technicolor measles.

The machine really got going. It painted not one picture but several. When the Professor did not feed canvases into it, it stretched out brush-holding arms and grabbed them. It painted pictures on top of Mr Palette-Brushleigh's pictures. It painted a portrait of the Mayor on the face of Mr Palette-Brushleigh. It did still lifes on rapidly running spectators.

'Help!' shouted the onlookers. 'Switch it off!'

The Professor pulled levers and twiddled dials, but he guessed it would make no difference and it didn't.

'Some miscreants have sabotaged the machine,' gasped the Professor, receiving a country cottage on the forehead.

'To the rescue!' shouted Colonel Dedshott, who had taken the precaution of bringing some Catapult Cavaliers again.

'Man the lifeboats!' roared Commander Hardaport (Retired), who had come to see seascapes.

Slap, plop, squirt, whizzy dizzy splosh! went the machine, busily doing abstract paintings on the windows.

'Stop it!' 'Help!' 'Fire!' 'Police!' yelled the crowd.

Colonel Dedshott and the Catapult Cavaliers descended on the machine and were painted shocking pink and lime green in hexagons before they could get a blow in.

'Smash it!' yelled the Advanced Artists, retreating before a fusillade of ruined castles and picturesque cottages.

'Action stations!' roared Commander Hardaport (Retired), receiving a rough sea with rocks in the waist-coat as he launched himself in line ahead at the machine.

At last the machine ran out of paint and quietened down.

'Now's our chance to bust it!' yelled the Advanced Artists advancing threateningly.

'No, you don't, by Jove!' cried Colonel Dedshott. The rainbow-coloured Catapult Cavaliers lined up to protect the machine.

'I take over this machine in the Queen's name!' cried Colonel Dedshott, saluting with a rose madder hand. 'Invaluable and invincible weapon against future enemies of the realm!' he declared.

Then the Catapult Cavaliers hoisted the machine on their shoulders and marched left, right, left, right, out of the Gallery followed by Colonel Dedshott and cries from the leftish and rightish artists.

Next day Professor Branestawm received a very

military letter on buff paper from General Shatterfortz, thanking him for presenting his most formidable engine to the army and assuring him that few enemies would have the courage to face its barrage of artistic ammunition, and adding that he was having it converted to hurl pictures of tanks and fortresses instead of churches and country cottages.

5

Branestawm's Railway

PROFESSOR BRANESTAWM went into Great Pagwell
Station, put two large washers, in mistake for money, on
the little ticket-buying window, and said:

'Second class return, please.'

'Where to?' asked the ticket man.

'Why, er – to Great Pagwell,' said the Professor.

'But this *is* Great Pagwell,' said the ticket man.

'Yes, yes, I know,' said the Professor. 'That is where
I wish to return to.'

'But where do you want to go before you return?'
asked the ticket man, sitting down.

But the Professor couldn't remember where he
wanted to go, so he went out, leaving the washers on the
ticket window, and the ticket man dropped them into
a railway Metal Container, waste-paper for, though
metal washers didn't really come under the heading
of waste-paper within the meaning of the Railway
Act.

Outside the station the Vicar of Pagwell came beam-
ing up to the Professor.

'Ah, my dear Professor,' he said, 'I wonder if you can
help me. I have to go to Pagwell Parva every other
Sunday to conduct a service and there is no way of
getting there.'

'Um – ah, no, there isn't,' said the Professor. 'Unless
of course, you have a horse, like Colonel Dedshott,' he

added, 'or a bicycle, like Mrs Flittersnoop, or a car, like Dr Mumpzanmeazle.'

The Vicar's twin daughters, Maisie and Daisie, had a car, but the only time they took the Vicar to Pagwell Parva in it, they went so fast and scared him so much, he ran out of prayers before he got to the church. After that he used to walk, but it made him so tired he nearly fell asleep in the middle of his own sermon, which is very much against the rules.

'I thought you might be able to invent some kind of vehicular conveyance,' said the Vicar, 'as the railway does not, I fear, go there.'

At that moment a train gave an urgent whistle. The Professor hurriedly raised his hat to the Vicar and shot into the station, just in time to get on a train not going to the place he had just remembered he wanted to go to.

Eventually, the Professor got home, after changing trains three times and coming back by bus from where he had wanted to go, although he had not been able to remember, when he got there, what it was he had wanted to go there for. However, by that time he had the details of the *Professor Branestawm Great Pagwell and Pagwell Parva Railway* all worked out in the most precise confusion.

'I shall have a single line railway,' he explained to Colonel Dedshott, 'because one line is cheaper than two. It is – er – the same kind of idea as two heads being better than one,' he added.

'Ha!' said the Colonel, who reckoned that one head was one too many for listening to the Professor's explanations. 'But what about safety? Collisions, Branestawm. Can't have anything like that you know. Better to have line for each way, by Jove.'

'Tut tut, my dear Dedshott,' said the Professor. 'There will be no possibility of collisions because we shall have only one train.'

'Hrrumph, yes, of course,' grunted the Colonel, who reckoned there could always be the possibility of anything where the Professor was concerned.

The Professor had finally decided to have a sort of loop at each end of the railway so that the train could go round the loop and come back on the same line.

As the P.B.G.P. & P.P.R. – *Professor Branestawm Great Pagwell and Pagwell Parva Railway* – began to get up steam, so to speak, everybody became very helpful. The gas company gave the remains of two and a half traction engines they had no further use for and which were making the gas works look untidy. And of course, that got the Professor off to a lovely steamy start with his railway engine. British Rail, who felt a bit red about the ears through not having a railway to Pagwell Parva themselves, gave the Professor no end of railway lines taken from places they didn't see why they should go to any more. And they lent him rows and rows of working-on-the-line men – the ones you aren't supposed to throw out of the window anything likely to hurt – to help lay the line.

The Professor went along to see the Pagwell Council.

'Where is this railway going to run?' asked one of the Pagwell Councillors, who didn't agree with anything new happening.

'We can't have it along the road,' said the Roads, Highways and Public Footpaths man.

'It must not come anywhere near my garden,' cried

the Mayor, who had only just escaped having a motor-
way through his drawing-room.

'Pray do not be alarmed,' said the Professor in his
most soothing voice, doing a complicated juggling act
with his five pairs of spectacles, three rolls of plans, six
encouraging letters, and a cup of tea which the Mayor's
secretary had brought him. 'The owners of the land
over which the railway will – ah – run have been most
kind.'

They certainly had. Farmer Plownough, who owned
a substantial field in the right place, said he didn't
mind them having their railway across it. 'But,' he
warned them, 'if that there train o' yours gets knocked
down by one o' my old cows, well then, that ain't no
fault of mine, remember.'

The rest of the land between Great Pagwell and
Pagwell Parva belonged to Lord Pagwell, who owned
the Pagwell Publishing Company. As he was a very kind
gentleman who liked letting people do things, there was
no difficulty at all about a little thing like running a
railway line, with trimmings, across his land.

But there was still a bit of a to-do with Pagwell
Council about safety measures. The Traffic man, who
had been terrified of accidents ever since he nearly
knocked down a policeman on his bicycle, wanted a
man with a red flag to walk ahead of the train. But when
somebody said, 'But suppose the train knocks down the
man with the red flag?' the Traffic Councillor
hurriedly grabbed up his papers and went to lunch.

Lunchtime reminded the Professor that all proper
railways have restaurant cars, and so he shot off home
to discuss this matter with Mrs Flittersnoop, who knew
a great deal about meals and was frightfully clever at

producing them even under the most discouraging
conditions.

'Well, I'm sure, sir, I've never run a restaurant car
before,' she said. 'But you never know what you can do
till you try, so if you say so, sir, well, indeed, I'll do my
best.'

The Professor did his best too, and so did Miss
Frenzie of the Pagwell Publishing Company, and
between them they worked out a nice suitable menu for
the restaurant car. It included such delicacies as:

> Fishplate and chips
> Milk train pudding
> Bogies on toast
> Puff puff pastry
> Sandswitches
> Bridge rolls
> Tender steak
> Steamed tunnels
> Junction junket
> Apple freighters
> and
> Expressed coffee.

'We must, of course, have a civic send-off for your
railway, Professor,' said the Mayor, who was a great
one for having Civic Occasions as often as possible,
preferably with plenty of refreshments to go with them.

So while the Professor was getting the train finished,
Mrs Flittersnoop, assisted by her sister Aggie and egged
on by Miss Frenzie, in between rapid dashes to distant
parts of the country on Pagwell Book Company business, got ready for a really slap-up lunch in the restaurant car. And the Pagwell tradesmen gave no end of
things for the sake of the advertisement, though some of

them were a bit difficult to fit into the lunch menu. Things like ten pounds of assorted nails from the Pagwell Hardware Store and four tons of coal from the Pagwell Paraffin, Coal, Coke and Firewood Shop. But the Professor managed to use up the nails in making the train; while the coal, which wasn't any use for the engine as it burned a special kind of fuel invented by the Professor, was stacked in neat heaps by the line and helped it to look like a real railway.

At last the train was finished, and highly magnificent it looked.

It had a funnel six feet high with a brass band round the top that made it look as if the engine was smiling. It had buffers sticking out of a nice red strip at the front. It had a great many wheels of various sizes, two steam domes on its back, which made it look slightly like a Bactrian camel, except that camels don't usually have P.B.G.P. & P.P.R. in gold letters on their sides. It also had a name, the Pagwell Flyer, which was a bit optimistic, though that was just as well for the people in the restaurant car who were having to cope with soup and somewhat easily spillable Railway Hotpot. And the line was a bit wavy in places because it went over some fences Lord Pagwell didn't want pulled down and round some bushes he didn't want dug up.

'I think we should arrange to entertain the passengers on the first run to tea at Parva Towers,' said Lord Pagwell. It was his country residence and he was very proud of it. It had once been a water mill, and, although the water wheel didn't go round any more as most of it had not been there for a century or so, the water went charging past in no end of a hurry and the mill race was very useful to Lord Pagwell's cook. She managed to get

it to do the washing-up very satisfactorily by putting
the dishes carefully in upstream, running round the
not-working wheel and taking them out nice and clean
on the other side, sometimes with a fish or two in the
saucepans, which came in very handy next dinner-time.

Inside Parva Towers was one room full of mechanical
armchairs which Professor Branestawm had invented
for his Lordship. They rocked you to and fro, or jigged
you up and down, or swung you in exhilarating circles,
according to what sort of sitting-down exercise you
fancied.

Then there was another room containing astonishing
clocks, all of which told a different time; so there were
usually several of them striking and chiming at once.
And there was one specially tall, skinny grandfather
clock that was so high it had to have a hole cut in the
ceiling for it, and it told the time in the spare bedroom.

But Lord and Lady Pagwell only stayed there for a
day or two occasionally, when Lord Pagwell couldn't
stand the buses hurtling past the office window or Miss
Frenzie hurtling in and out of the office doors. And
when Lady Pagwell wanted to get away from the shops
which always induced her to spend a great deal more
money than she intended, mostly on things she certainly
didn't need, couldn't really afford, but simply had to
have.

The great day of the civic start-off of the first run of
the Pagwell Flyer was fine and sunny.

'Thank goodness, I'm sure, sir,' said Mrs Flittersnoop, who was afraid the carriages might leak if it
rained.

The train was drawn up at the special station built

for it, which you could hardly see for flags and bunting and most of the population of Great Pagwell, who had got the day off by the most ingenious excuses.

Colonel Dedshott's Catapult Cavaliers, by kind permission of General Shatterfortz, were drawn up in very nearly straight lines. The Mayor and Council were in their robes, which made them a tight fit in the carriages. Mrs Flittersnoop, her sister Aggie, Miss Frenzie, several of sister Aggie's relatives and one or two of Miss Frenzie's staff, all in their best clothes and wearing little aprons with P.B.G.P. & P.P.R. embroidered on them were drawn up in the restaurant car, all ready for railway appetites.

The Vicar's identical twin daughters were at the ticket office, Daisie at Great Pagwell Station and Maisie at Pagwell Parva Station (or else the other way round), which was going to be a bit confusing for passengers, who would find it difficult to remember whether they were coming or going.

Professor Branestawm, of course, was going to drive the engine, and he wore a suit of dungarees with five pockets for his pairs of spectacles and an engine driver's hat on the right way round.

Colonel Dedshott, leaving command of the Catapult Cavaliers to his deputy, Major Shoobang, was acting as guard. He wore a railway guard's hat instead of his usual plumed one, carried red and green flags and a whistle, and had his horse with him in a special horse compartment that let the horse put his head out of the window to enjoy the view.

'I declare the *Professor Branestawm Great Pagwell and Pagwell Parva Railway* open,' cried the Mayor, and retired to the restaurant car to restore his strength, after saying all that name, with Flittersnoop and Frenzie steak pudding.

The Pagwell Flyer emitted a burst of pale green steam, hissed like a troup of indignant swans, and its wheels began to go round.

'Hurray!' cried everyone.

'Right away!' yelled Colonel Dedshott, waving both red and green flags together.

And away rumbled the Flyer with the people waving and cheering, and Farmer Plownough's cows looking on in astonishment and hoping this wasn't a new kind of gadget for milking them.

Meanwhile, the inhabitants of Pagwell Parva were all out in *their* best clothes, some of which didn't fit very well as they hadn't been worn for ages. A man was posted on top of Pagwell Towers with a telescope to let everyone know when the Flyer was sighted. But he forgot to take the little lid off the end of the telescope so that everywhere looked like the middle of the night. Fortunately it didn't matter as you could hear the Pagwell Flyer coming several miles off.

The Pagwell Town Band got to its feet and began to play the Pagwell Flyer in. The sound was magnificent. Not all the bandsmen played the same tune, but no one worried because the Pagwell Flyer made such a hissing and clanking and puffing and whirring that not all the massed Guards' bands and symphony orchestras in the world going full blast could have made themselves heard.

Clank, clank, boom, zzzz, splang. The Pagwell Flyer stopped almost at the station in a cloud of steam and dust.

'A most successful journey,' said the Professor, taking off all his five pairs of spectacles but leaving on a variety of dirty smudges the Pagwell Flyer had been good enough to give him.

Lord and Lady Pagwell came out of Parva Towers to greet them and all the important people went in to have a Train-Warming Tea on the lawn. It was very exclusive as the lawn was only three yards square and, even with Colonel Dedshott's horse boarded out to have his tea in the next field, there wasn't much room to stick out your finger politely while drinking tea.

The rest of the passengers had no end of a time deciding which of Pagwell Parva's tea gardens to go to. Some very fast feeders managed to have tea at two or three of them.

There was Rose Cottage, which had no roses, but plenty of marigolds. Next door was The Old Stone House, built partly of brick and partly of wood. There was Riverside Tea Gardens, which wasn't exactly at the side of the river, but you could see the water quite easily if you stood on a chair, and it was a clear day, and the people opposite had cut their hedge and didn't have enormous washing hanging out. Then there was the Parva Arms, which was really an inn, but you could get a whale of a tea there, including meat pies and a kind of plump sausage called Parva Polony. You could also have home-brewed ginger beer instead of tea. It was lovely and frothy, and went up your nose and made you sneeze unless you approached it very cautiously and got the first drink out of the glass before it saw you coming.

Pagwell Parva was a great shopping centre. Not that there were any shops, because there weren't. But you could buy most things from the villagers: bread and butter that tasted better than cake; a special celebrated Parva Cake that tasted like nothing on earth and was absolutely irresistible; and there was Parva Porridge that was so robust that you had to eat it with a knife and fork. That was very convenient really because you could buy a sheet of it, roll it up and take it home, instead of eating it on the spot, which you didn't really want to do in the afternoon as porridge isn't a tea-time food.

By the time everyone had finished their souvenir buying, and teas, and flower admiring, Professor Branestawm reckoned it was time to start back, in case it took a bit longer through being uphill part of the way. So off went the whistle again, and soon everybody was

crammed on board and the Pagwell Flyer was roaring
back to Great Pagwell.

'Very satisfactory,' said the Professor, waggling
levers and opening valves and adjusting pressures, while
little dials went round and round, and up and down,
and to and fro.

'The Professor is to be congratulated,' purred the
Vicar, thinking how nice it was going to be to sit in a
railway carriage and compose uplifting sermons on the
way to Pagwell Parva church, with no physical efforts
involved.

'Yes,' said one of the Pagwell Councillors, 'and the
more so, if I may say so, because this time for a change
nothing has gone wrong with the Professor's invention.'

Just then the train went over a bumpy bit of railway
and the thing connecting the engine to the carriages
snapped.

'Um – well, never mind,' said the Professor. 'As we
are nearly at Great Pagwell, the carriages will have
sufficient – ah – momentum to carry them to the plat-
form and I can stop them by applying the brakes on the
engine at the appropriate moment.'

Then suddenly the engine began gaining on the
carriages. Wider and wider grew the gap. 'Oh my
goodness!' gasped the Professor.

'I shall apply the brakes,' he said, applying them.
But the engine didn't slow down, it went faster.

Then they came to a downhill part and the carriages
gathered speed.

'Doing a nice pace,' said Doctor Mumpzanmeazle,
as trees, cows, fences and other agricultural scenery
shot by.

Faster and faster went the carriages. But still faster went the engine. Pagwell Flyer they had called it, and Flyer it was going to be.

Professor Branestawm turned steam-shutting-off wheels. The engine went still faster. He pulled slowing-down levers and added another six miles an hour to the engine's speed.

Things were extra awful. Colonel Dedshott, who always rescued the Professor from his inventions, was at the other end of the train in the guard's van. And the Catapult Cavaliers were no help either. They were still drawn up at Great Pagwell Station ready to welcome the train back.

But Colonel Dedshott was used to the Professor's inventions. He reckoned it was past time for this one to go wrong.

'Going too fast, by Jove!' he cried. 'Must be something wrong. Branestawm may need help.'

He leapt out of the guard's van, and his horse leapt off the train. They both fell over. The Colonel scrambled into the saddle.

'My word!' he gasped. 'Engine running away! To the rescue!'

Cloppety cloppety clop, the Colonel's horse tore after the engine.

Diddley dum, diddley dum, the engine roared away from the Colonel.

But hurray, the Colonel was gaining on the engine! He reached it. His horse took it at a bound, soaring over it as if it were a two-inch high fence.

'Whoa!' cried the Colonel. 'Too far, by Jove!' He wheeled the horse round and galloped after the engine again. He caught up with it.

'Branestawm!' he cried, galloping along beside the engine. 'Something wrong? Can I help?'

'Ah, my dear Dedshott, have the goodness to step aboard,' panted the Professor, not forgetting his manners even in the midst of dire emergency and lever-pulling.

The Colonel grabbed hold of a bit of engine and swung himself on beside the Professor. His horse went off after a juicy bit of grass and the Colonel and the Professor set about getting the engine stopped.

'Halt! As you were there!' growled the Colonel, thinking perhaps the engine might understand military language. He aimed a shot from his catapult into the engine's inside, which made no difference. He took off his jacket and stuffed it into the firebox to put the flames out. The engine swallowed it whole and blew it out of its funnel encircled by green and mauve smoke and illuminated stars.

'Here's the train coming back!' cried the Great Pagwellians, gathered on the station to welcome it home. But the engine, with Professor Branestawm and the Colonel doing everything they knew, and several things they didn't know, to stop it, shot past in clouds of multi-coloured steam and assorted train noises.

'Where's the train?' cried everyone.

'Here she is!' called someone else.

The carriages appeared, rattling along at goodness knows how many miles an hour.

'Why aren't we stopping?' asked Dr Mumpzanmeazle, getting his doctor's case off the rack in case there was going to be an accident.

'I fear this is somewhat irregular,' said the Vicar, as his church shot past the window at high speed.

'Must stop the engine!' gasped the Professor. He pulled eight levers at once. Three came off in his hand. The Pagwell Flyer zoomed down the last bit of rail and round the loop.

'The engine's coming back for her!' cried the Pagwellians.

The engine went right round the loop and came charging back, smack into the carriages. A collision on a single line with only one train!

But, thank goodness, nobody was hurt. Because as the line went downhill to the loop the engine had to come uphill coming back from it. And it was probably a bit tired from the journey. So the collision occurred with a none-too-resounding crash and no damage was done, except for one cracked teacup smashed beyond repair in the restaurant car, and the Mayor's chain of office thrown out of the window, though fortunately there were no men working on the line it could hurt.

But that was the end of Professor Branestawm's railway after only one glorious trip, returning same day. The East Pagwell Fairground and Roundabout Company bought the railway, pulled up the lines and relaid them in a circle, and kept the train going round and round, after getting the engine into stoppable condition again. They charged fifteen new pence a go to ride on it. And the restaurant car was set up at the side of the track and called 'The Railway Cafe' and did a roaring trade in stationary refreshments of all kinds.

'I think perhaps it is just as well my railway did not last,' said the Professor over tea in the nice quiet non-moving sitting room at the Vicar's. 'Because you see,' he began ticking off points on his fingers, 'the railway would have brought a lot of people to Pagwell Parva for the country delights. That would have caused many cafes and shops and cinemas to be built in Pagwell Parva to cater for the tourist trade. You follow me, Vicar?'

'Ah yes, my dear Professor,' said the Vicar, thanking goodness he had managed to find a nice, talkative curate for the Pagwell Parva church, who would do the services for him.

'Well, then,' went on the Professor, 'once that – er – happened Pagwell Parva would soon become so much like Great Pagwell there would really be no point in people going there.'

'Ah,' said the Vicar, 'so now we have the most extraordinary situation that as long as one cannot get to

Pagwell Parva everybody wants to go there, but once it becomes easy to get there nobody wants to go.'

'Precisely,' said the Professor.

But he was still the only man to achieve a collision on a railway with only one train, and that was jolly well something.

6

Branestawmy Weather

'OH, BOTHER IT!' said Dr Mumpzanmeazle in a very dark brown medicine sort of voice. 'Really, this is *too* much.'

'Dear, oh dearie me!' exclaimed Mrs Flittersnoop, 'this is so vexing, and me with a big wash to do.'

'Hrrmph!' snorted Colonel Dedshott.

'This is really most inconvenient,' murmured the Vicar.

'I – um – ah – think it is time something was done about it,' said Professor Branestawm.

Rain was coming down all over the Pagwells. The raindrops bounced off the roofs, they slid down the rhubarb leaves, they splashed into bird baths, which was a waste of their time because the bird baths were already full and anyway the birds were getting too many baths from the rain to want to bother with any more. Everywhere looked as if people had been ruling slanting lines across it. It was a real soaker. And it had been going on for days, in spite of the weather forecasts of dry spells and occasional outbreaks of sunshine.

'I fear it is a very poor outlook for the Church Bazaar which is due shortly,' said the Vicar, who was having tea with the Professor, partly because he liked talking to him and partly because he liked Mrs Flittersnoop's home-made currant cake. 'Can't you invent some sort of machine to give us some sunshine?' he asked the Professor.

Professor Branestawm lifted his slice of cake and took one of his pairs of spectacles from under it. 'The idea had occurred to me,' he said. 'A machine to control the weather. Impossible, of course, but it has interesting possibilities. I shall give it some thought.' He stood up and put all his spectacles in his pocket.

'I really must be going now,' he said. 'Thank you for a most enjoyable tea, Vicar.' And, thinking he was at the Vicar's instead of the other way round, he went out, taking his umbrella from the umbrella stand.

It had stopped raining by the time the Professor's Weather Managing Machine was ready for action, which was just as well because, apart from the bits the Professor was wearing, it was a very outdoor sort of machine, with long, skinny rods going up and up and quantities of tall towers held up by slanting wires. But the sky was still full of excessively murky clouds.

'Only dirty clouds make rain,' said the Professor, conducting the Vicar on a tour of the works, 'so the first – er – ah – purpose of my invention is to wash the clouds by means of electronic projected detergents of a special type.'

'Indeed, yes, I suppose,' said the Vicar.

'Jolly clever, Branestawm, my word!' cried Colonel Dedshott, who had come along to see what kind of arrangement it was that he might have to deal with if it got out of hand. Not that the Colonel minded much about weather, being a soldier. He always reckoned it was a case of on parade on time and are we going to let the British Army be daunted by a spot of rain, not likely, by Jove!

'These dials,' said the Professor, pointing to alarm clock arrangements, 'enable me to confine my chosen weather to any particular area.'

'Such as the Vicarage lawn,' murmured the Vicar, thinking of his Church Bazaar.

'Here we have the cloud-cleansing columns,' went on the Professor, 'the rain-removing rhomboids, the sun switches and the wind-winding winches.' He stacked his spectacles on top of his head and swung round to another part of the machine while Colonel Dedshott prodded something with his sword.

'What's that, eh Branestawm?' he said. 'Fine weather parader, what?' The Colonel's idea of controlling the weather was to line up the various kinds, number them off, march away those not wanted and tell the others to carry on.

'Er – ah – pardon me – Dedshott,' fussed the Professor, hurriedly pushing the sword aside. 'That is the thunder button. Have the goodness not to press it while I am talking.' He pointed to rows of other buttons, lots of levers and several switches. 'And there we have the lightning levers, and hailstorm handles, the snow strainers and the hurricane adjustment modules.' He put on his looking-over-the-top-of spectacles and said, 'With this machine, gentlemen, I think we have the means to provide whatever may be required in the way of weather, in any – um – ah – particular place at any particular time.'

'But surely,' protested the Vicar, who was beginning to feel a bit doubtful whether all this bossing about of the weather was something he ought to agree with, 'surely, nobody will want thunderstorms or snow or disagreeable weather of that kind?'

'It is not merely a matter of providing the weather we want,' the Professor explained. 'We must also be prepared to take avoiding action against the weather we do not want. With my machine it is just as possible to switch off undesirable weather as to switch it on.

'Now, this map,' he went on, pointing to a diagram that looked like two bent lamb chops and a mountain of knobbly spinach, 'covers the area of Great Pagwell and the surrounding places. This,' he pointed with the back end of a pair of spectacles at a triangular blob of spinach with a bit out of it, 'is where we are at present. So I set the pointer to this spot as we are going to control the weather overhead.'

As he spoke a particularly grubby portion of cloud let go a collection of heavy raindrops it had no further use for.

'I shall now direct the cloud-cleansing columns,' said the Professor, 'then activate the rain-removing rhomboids, and switch on the sun.' He pulled down a large brass lever. Hummings occurred. The air went all wiggly as if someone was shaking it like a rug.

'Why, bless me!' cried the Vicar, not believing it.

The dirty clouds began to crumble up. The black parts faded away as if someone were washing them with a special instant detergent.

'Why, if the clouds aren't getting quite white!' cried Mrs Flittersnoop.

'And now they're gradually fading away!' said the Vicar.

Peep, peep, peep, pippety peep, went the weather machine. The clouds, now as clean as a new white handkerchief, started coming apart at the seams. Bits floated off here and there. Soon there were none left and the sun came gleaming out all golden and warm and summery.

'Well I never!' said Mrs Flittersnoop, and the Colonel and the Vicar both cried, 'Congratulations, Branestawm!'

Then the Professor switched off the machine. They left the sunshine to look after itself, which it did very well, and they all went in for glasses of lemonade and slices of the famous Flittersnoop currant cake.

That afternoon the Professor was busy setting his weather machine for (a) a nice calm sunny day for the Church Bazaar, (b) some gentle growing rain for Farmer Plownough's crops, (c) a helping of brisk wind for the Pagwell sailing races on Pagwell Canal and (d) a reasonably cool day for the Grand Parade of the Catapult Cavaliers to celebrate General Shatterfortz's birthday, so that none of the soldiers should faint and make the place look untidy. And as all these pieces of weather happily had to occur at different places at different times, all was well.

'I think we should give the Professor the Freedom of the Pagwells for this great public service,' said the Mayor.

'I reckon he's already got it,' said the Town Clerk, who had a shop that sold sunshades and was wondering if he could get the Professor to come in with him on the business so as to make sure of profitable weather.

The following week a thunderstorm occurred in the middle of the West Pagwell Flower Show and there was a fall of purple snow on North Pagwell Racecourse which made it difficult to discover which horse had won as all the jockeys looked the same colour.

'Dear, dear!' said the Professor, looking at his machine rather severely, 'I fear that, in shunting the

thunderstorm away from the Church Bazaar last week,
I – um – ah – permitted a build-up of electrical disturb-
ance which I had not noticed, over the Flower Show.'

'What about the purple snow, what?' demanded
Colonel Dedshott, who didn't agree with mauve
horses.

'There is the question of the accumulation of unwanted weather types,' said the Professor, 'which have
to be dispelled over areas where they will do no harm.'
He pulled a lever which sidetracked a heavy hailstorm
accompanied by high winds from a football match
between Upper Pagwell Dromedaries and Pagwell-on-
the-Hill Billies, and brought it down instead on Pagwell
Moor during the night.

'But are you sure there is no danger attached to this
interference with the ways of nature, my dear Professor?' said the Vicar.

'Oh, no, no, Vicar, no danger at all,' the Professor
assured him. 'Though I must admit,' he added, 'that it
is sometimes a little difficult to find space in the atmos-
phere for various types of unwanted weather.'

It certainly was. The higher air over the Pagwells
where the Professor had banished them was becoming
littered with unwanted thunderstorms queuing up to
occur, with not-required snow waiting to fall and
quantities of hail saved up for a haily day.

Everybody who had heard of the Professor's wonderful weather machine started sending in requests.

'Can we have a fine day on Saturday for the Pagwell
Picnic Union's outing?' asked a pleading letter.

'Please arrange snow on Saturday for photograph-
ing,' said a telegram from the Christmas Card Photo-
graphers Society.

People wanted totally different kinds of weather in the same place on the same day. The Professor's head began to go round and round like Colonel Dedshott's.

'I don't think they should do it, sir,' said Mrs Flittersnoop. 'All this expecting the kind of weather they like and never mind what anybody else wants.'

But the Professor wasn't going to be daunted. Wasn't he the great tamer of tempests, the unconquerable producer of simultaneous sunshine? He pulled more levers and twiddled innumerable dials.

Then the trouble really began.

Five kinds of assorted weather broke out over Pagwell Town Háll. Snow in Lower Pagwell was followed immediately by hot sunshine, followed by more snow, then alternate snow and sun, so that people found themselves out in the hot sun with snow shovels and wearing bikinis in ten-foot snowdrifts.

'This is what comes of usurping the authority of the B.B.C.,' complained a weather forecasting man.

Pink and green hail. Rain came down boiling hot and people made cocoa with it but had to wear asbestos overcoats so as not to get scalded. Exploding hailstones went *ping* or *pong* according to whether they were right or left-handed hailstones. There were thunderstorms with knotted lightning and swing beat thunder.

The B.B.C. gave up forecasting the weather because they never knew what the Professor was going to do next.

The flowers and fruit became so confused at assorted weather taking place without warning that the roses came out in the middle of the night and fell to bits at breakfast-time. Strawberries started growing on apple trees, there were gooseberries the size of marrows and tiny marrows in bunches like grapes, while some varieties of creeper refused to creep and grew straight down into the earth instead of up.

The weather became so changeable that the only possible costume for going out in was a fur-lined bathing costume and snowshoes, with a heavy mackintosh and a sunshade.

'I feel I should summon assistance,' gasped the Professor, pulling levers which immediately became unpulled. 'Mrs Flittersnoop, kindly telephone to Colonel

Dedshott for help.' He spun three dials which spun
back. Switches began going on and off by themselves.
The air shook with storms and sunshine, with high
velocity winds, deep depressions, cold fronts and balmy
sunshine.

'Help!' cried the Professor.

'Branestawm! To the rescue!' came a welcome shout.
Colonel Dedshott galloped up to the inventory door
with snow on his boots and sunburn on his face. The
Catapult Cavaliers, the Pagwell Fire Brigade, the Boy
Scouts and the Girls' Friendly Society came tearing up,
on horses, in fire engines, on bicycles and scooters and
fairy cycles, and on foot.

Everyone got soaking wet in two seconds and bone
dry again in another three. *Crash! Bang!* The Cavaliers
set about the weather machine. The weather machine
set about the Fire Brigade. The Boy Scouts tried to do
the machine a good turn but it spat red hot hail at
them.

'Oh, dearie me, whatever is it all coming to?'
wailed Mrs Flittersnoop. She would have gone to stay
with her sister Aggie, but sister Aggie's spare bedroom
had blown inside out.

Crash! Boom! Hiss! Catapult Cavaliers were catapult-
ed here and there by mad tornadoes. 'At 'em, boys!'
'My word, Branestawm!' 'Tut, I fear this has got a
little out of hand.'

Then suddenly help arrived from where no one
expected it.

A thunderstorm sailed up overhead and the weather
machine was struck by lightning! It was hit in the same
place five times and in five different places once each.
The cloud-cleansing columns were crashily collapsed.

The rain-removing rhomboids were firmly removed, the sun switches sorted out and the wind-winding winches wound up. Then the wreckage was covered in striped hail and buried in spotted snow, and at last up came a hurricane and blew the whole lot into the deepest part of Pagwell Lake from where it was fortunately never recovered.

'Well, er, thank goodness that's over,' said the Professor, as he and the Colonel and the Cavaliers and the Fire Brigade and the Scouts and the Friendly Girls all sat down to a well-earned meal of cocoa with slices of snow-covered currant cake.

Mrs Flittersnoop turned on the television. On the screen appeared a gentleman still covered in snow.

'Here is the weather forecast,' he said, and the set blew up.

7

Branestawm's Zoo

PROFESSOR BRANESTAWM went into the kitchen to speak to Mrs Flittersnoop, but as soon as he got inside the door he forgot what it was he was going to speak to her about. Not that there was anything unusual in that. But this time it wasn't a half-thought-of invention that caused the Professor to forget; it was an enormous, smooth dog lying on the hearthrug and being used as a cushion by Mrs Flittersnoop's cat.

'I hope you'll forgive the liberty, sir,' said Mrs Flittersnoop, looking up from a shepherd's pie she was making, 'but my cousin Hetty asked me if I'd be good enough to look after Tiny while she and the children are on holiday. It seems they're going in a caravan, sir,' she added, 'and there wouldn't be room for Tiny.'

'Er – um – ah – yes, of course,' said the Professor, quite seeing that there wouldn't be room for Tiny in a caravan, as there wasn't room for him in the kitchen. Or at least it would be more correct to say there wasn't room for Mrs Flittersnoop now that Tiny was there. But she'd pushed the table up against the wall and was making an extra narrow shepherd's pie so as to manage.

'He seems a very – ah – nice dog,' said the Professor, looking at Tiny through various pairs of spectacles in the hope that he'd look a little smaller through some of them, but he didn't.

'Brrrrmph,' said Tiny, stretching himself luxuriously.

'I have no doubt I shall be able to invent some ways of amusing him,' said the Professor, and went to look up some books on amusing dogs though Tiny seemed to find it quite amusing enough being a cushion on the hearthrug.

While the Professor was on his way to his inventory the front doorbell rang. It was the Vicar, accompanied by a small shaggy dog with a lot of teeth.

'Ah, good morning, my dear Professor,' said the Vicar. 'I wonder whether you would be so kind as to look after Esau for a time. My wife and I are spending a few weeks with some friends who do not like dogs.'

'Grr wark!' snorted Esau, and shot past the Professor into the kitchen, saw Mrs Flittersnoop's cat and decided to chase it. Tiny, released from his duties as cushion, ate the shepherd's pie Mrs Flittersnoop was making for the Professor's dinner, though as he wasn't a sheep dog he shouldn't have, and went to sleep again.

Mrs Flittersnoop's cat and Esau were on their third lap of the garden and so equally spaced that it was difficult to see who was chasing whom and neither of them could remember, when a black and white naval-looking cat belonging to Commander Hardaport (Retired) next door up-anchored and joined in without waiting to decide whether he was chasing Esau or the other cat.

'Ha, Professor!' shouted the Commander. 'Glad to see the Admiral has taken a fancy to your place. Wanted to ask you to look after him. I'm off for a yachting holiday and cats don't care for yachting, you know. Too much water and all that. Thanks awfully.' He saluted and stumped into his Commander's cabin to send off urgent messages about ropes and things connected with his holiday.

'I – um – ah, it really seems to me,' said the Professor as Esau, the Admiral and Mrs Flittersnoop's cat came through the dining-room window and sat in a row with tongues hanging out, waiting for refreshment, 'I mean, can we – er – manage with all these animals?'

'Well, I'm sure sir, it is a bit more than I expected,' agreed Mrs Flitternsoop.

Just then Lord Pagwell turned up with a budgie in a very fancy cage, and gave careful, very long and extremely complicated directions for looking after him while he and Lady Pagwell were away at their villa on Lake Como. He had hardly left before Miss Frenzie arrived accompanied by an absolute clump of children from Pagwell Grammar School who in turn were accompanied by a hamster, two white mice, a parrot, a multi-coloured goat, three grass snakes, a mynah bird and a puffin.

'Ah, *there* you are, my dear man,' said Miss Frenzie, 'sorry to rush you like this, but *do* be a dear and cope with these sweet little pets while I take the children for the annual camp organized by the Pagwell Publishing Company in the North of Scotland, thanks so much. Be seeing you.'

The entire company went whistling off up the road leaving the Professor surrounded by things on legs and things with wings and things with neither.

'Oh, my goodness!' cried the Professor. 'I – er – really – no, no!' Then he saw a horse coming through the gate.

'No, no, no, no!' he squealed. 'Not horses! We can't take horses, no, not really, we can't!'

But it was only Colonel Dedshott, on his horse.

'Ha! starting a zoo, Branestawm?' he cried.

He got off his horse which set to work on the Professor's privet hedge, where he was joined with some enthusiasm by the goat.

Before the Professor could reply, a circus procession began to go by on its way to Great Pagwell and when the Professor caught sight of eight elephants, two lions in a cage and twelve black Arabian steeds, he swept all the Grammar School girls' pets and Colonel Dedshott into the house and locked the door, to make sure the circus didn't start asking him to look after all those.

'I hear that dear Professor Branestawm is being kind enough to look after people's pets while they're away,' said a sweet old lady from Pagwell Gardens to three of her friends over tea and tarts at Ye Olde Bun Shoppe.

'Did you know Professor Branestawm is minding pets for people?' said the school teachers of East, West, North, South, Upper and Lower Pagwells to one another.

The news shot round faster than a bit of scandal and soon the Professor and Mrs Flittersnoop were submerged in animal, bird and reptile life of all kinds.

'I – ah – really don't know what we are to do with all these – er – these – er – creatures,' groaned the Professor, gazing frantically at a monkey who was hanging by his tail from the top of the inventory.

'Well, it's a blessing it won't be for long, sir,' said Mrs Flittersnoop. 'The owners will be fetching them back when they return from their holidays, I'm sure, sir.'

But either some people had very long holidays or else some people weren't so anxious to have their pets back as they might have been. For practically nobody came to collect their pets. Nobody, that is, except the Vicar who carried off Esau, still snarling, Commander Hardaport (Retired) who whistled the Admiral back aboard, and Miss Frenzie and her shoal of children, who swept up those of their pets they could pick out from the collection.

'This is terrible,' muttered Professor Branestawm. He was at breakfast with a parrot sitting on each shoulder, a kitten sitting on his plate waiting for kippers, an Alsatian and three Yorkshire terriers sitting under the table and a cow leaning against the sideboard.

'Don't forget you've to change your library books today, sir,' said Mrs Flittersnoop, giving the Professor a plateful of Kittie's Favourite Meat Cubes in mistake for his sausage.

'Ah yes, of course, ah – um – good gracious!' exclaimed the Professor. Mention of library books had suddenly launched a forty horsepower idea at him.

'Mrs Flittersnoop!' he cried. 'Mrs Flittersnoop, I see what we can do with all these pets!'

'Indeed, sir?' said Mrs Flittersnoop, who reckoned she could tell the owners what they could do with them if it came to that.

'A library!' cried the Professor, standing up and tipping a lapful of guinea pigs into the waste-paper basket. 'A pet library. A wonderful idea! Never been done before, as far as I know. Ring up Colonel Dedshott, Mrs Flittersnoop, and ask him to come round post haste. We must arrange details. I shall need help.'

'Ha yes, jolly clever!' said Colonel Dedshott, sitting

on an empty soda water bottle box as it was the only thing not already covered in assorted pets.

'You see the idea, Dedshott?' said the Professor, waving hands and spectacles and odd birds and things that happened to be clinging to him. 'People like to have pets but they do not always want them all the time, if you follow me. So my idea is to lend these – um – ah – creatures out by the week, rather like library books, only entirely different, and the money they pay for borrowing them will go towards buying food for the ones they don't take. Do I make myself clear? I thought perhaps you might get some of your Catapult Cavaliers to lend me a hand,' he added, 'giving the pets out you know, keeping a note of who has what, and when they should be returned.'

'Hrrrrmph!' said the Colonel.

Professor Branestawm's Pet Borrowing Zoolibrary was going full blast. Colonel Dedshott and his Catapult Cavaliers had got all the birds and animals and things neatly lined up in comfortable cages the Professor had made from disused boxes and not-required cartons and finished-with containers the manager of Pagwell Supermarket had been delighted to supply as a gesture to the Professor's work for homeless animals and birds, and also as a convenient way of getting rid of the things.

The mynah bird, who had been left behind by Miss Frenzie's schoolgirls and who was good at learning from soldiers, marched up and down the row of cages shouting, 'Line up there. Heads back. Thumbs in line with the seams of your trousers!'

The Professor invented a cat-stroking machine as there were far too many cats to be stroked adequately

by hand. He invented a dog-feeding machine that rang a bell and stopped feeding them when the dogs had had what the machine thought was enough. But some of the dogs were rather crafty and put their paws on the lid of the feeding bowl to keep it open after the bell rang.

Business was brisk and plentiful. People came from all the Pagwells and from miles outside, some to borrow pets and some to see the collection, which was better than a zoo in some ways and a great deal more un-likely. And Colonel Dedshott collected money from the people who borrowed pets and also from those who didn't, as admission to the Zoolibrary.

'I – really think we have solved the problem,' said the Professor, as hamsters and parrots and dogs and cats and lizards and grass snakes and an odd cow or two were carried off by borrowers.

The fame of Branestawm's Pet Borrowing Zoolibrary resounded North, South, East and West and all places in between. Newspapers came out with headlines like,

'Professor treats pets like books. Open and shut case for Zoolibrary' and 'How to have a different pet every week. Ask Professor Branestawm'.

Lord Pagwell came to collect his budgie, which he always took to Board Meetings of the Pagwell Publishing Company because it could repeat to him afterwards what everybody had said, and saved him from taking notes. But it repeated so many alarming things it had heard the parrots saying that he wouldn't take it and went away instead with a nice quiet canary that wouldn't be likely to shock a dignified collection of directors too much.

Some of the pigeons, who were homing pigeons, came back of their own accord before they were due and the Bishop of Pagwell Magna hurriedly returned the mynah bird the Monday after he borrowed it because it gave a rather unsuitable sermon in the Cathedral that Sunday.

'Everything seems to be going very well,' said the Professor to Colonel Dedshott. 'No machinery to go wrong this time, Dedshott. I – er – fancy we have at last hit on a disaster-proof invention.'

'Don't speak too soon,' said the Colonel, taking seventy-five new pence in half-penny pieces from the members of Pagwell-under-Ware Monkey Club, who were borrowing several lizards and a canary as a change from monkeys.

But nothing went wrong at all. In fact everything went a tremendous lot righter than anybody could expect from a Branestawm invention. This invention, far from going wrong itself, proceeded in the most dignified fashion to put right what had gone wrong before without its help.

Because just as most of the people who had left pets with the Professor to take care of, hadn't collected them and so started everything, so the people who were borrowing the pets started not bringing them back. Perhaps it was because they forgot. Perhaps it was because they got so fond of the pets they just couldn't bear to part with them. Perhaps the pets themselves found their new homes a bit more private than the Zoolibrary. And perhaps some of them liked their new owners' cooking better than Mrs Flittersnoop's, who, although she did her best, found it a bit complicated coping with the mixed menu for all that livestock.

So gradually all the inhabitants of the Zoolibrary were taken out and not returned and the Professor and Mrs Flittersnoop were left in peace and alone. At least not quite alone. Mrs Flittersnoop's cousin Hetty decided she didn't want Tiny back again. And Tiny, who had been asleep the whole time except when he woke up and ate other people's dinners, was quite content to go on being a cushion for Mrs Flittersnoop's cat. And the only other inmate left was the mynah bird, which Colonel Dedshott took under his wing. He thought it would be rather useful to send on parade to drill the Catapult Cavaliers any time when he didn't particularly feel much like going himself.

8

The Pagwell Monster

'THERE IT GOES, just by those reeds.'

'No, no, it's down the other end, look, a great long neck with a head like a horse with horns.'

'I saw it leap out of the water, it must be half a mile long.'

'Whatever is it?'

'Wherever did it come from?'

'Oo-er!'

All the people of Lower Pagwell were gathered in an excited clump along the edge of Pagwell Lake looking for the monster.

Yes, Pagwell Lake had a monster. Or at least everybody thought so. And, after all, what Loch Ness thinks it can do, Lower Pagwell reckons it can do better.

'Well,' said Dr Mumpzanmeazle, 'if there is a monster, I hope there isn't more than one. We don't want them producing little monsters all over the place.'

'Can you have little monsters?' asked the Vicar.

'Ha, you certainly can,' grunted Mr Stinckz-Bernagh, the science master of Pagwell College. 'I have some of them in my class.'

As a matter of fact, it all started with some of the boys from Pagwell College who thought it would be a kick or two to have a monster. So they rigged something up with old motor tyres, a long pole with an old sheet over it and a funny mask left over from the school pantomime. Then they launched it on the lake one dim and misty evening. It sank almost immediately, but kept bobbing up again in different parts of the lake.

'Jolly good, I reckon,' said a boy in a green jersey and orange-coloured hair.

'Let's go and tell people we've seen a monster,' cried a tall, thin boy with spectacles. And off they dashed.

Of course their parents didn't believe them. Parents are a bit like that.

'You imagined it,' said one of the fathers.

'One of your games, I'll be bound,' said a mum.

'Stuff and nonsense, monsters indeed!' said another.

But then the newspapers got hold of it and came out with placards saying, 'Mysterious Creature seen in Pagwell Lake. Is it the Loch Ness Monster come South?' and 'Beware of Pagwell Lake. Monster sighted.'

After that people went rushing down to the lake to see if they could see anything, and, of course, most of them did, whether there was anything to see or not.

One or two caught glimpses of the Pagwell College boys' monster when it bobbed up. One rather short-sighted man saw the Town Clerk's wife looking for the monster and thought she was it. Somebody else saw a horse and several cows standing in a line where the tail of the horse and the heads of the cows were hidden behind bushes or tree trunks or clumps of stuff, so that it looked like an enormously long animal with the head of a horse and the back part of a cow.

'Well I never, indeed, sir,' said Mrs Flittersnoop when she heard about it. 'A monster in Pagwell Lake! Do you think it can be, sir?'

'Ah, hum,' said Professor Branestawm, looking up monsters in various books. 'I shall go up to the attic,' he said. 'I can get a very good view of Pagwell Lake from there, and possibly I may see something to help solve this – er – mystery.'

He went up to the attic but got so interested in some ancient magazines, and old hats, and discarded mangles, and no-longer-wanted fire irons, and done-with things of all kinds, that he clean forgot about the monster.

Then Mrs Flittersnoop called to him that tea was ready and he looked up from some frightfully dusty copies of *The Train Spotters' Weekly* and his eye caught sight of the distant view of Pagwell Lake through the not very clean window.

'Good gracious!' he cried. 'This is most – er – ah – most – er – um –' He couldn't think what it was most, but he fiddled with his spectacles and had another look.

There, crawling out of Pagwell Lake, was the most monstrous monster he had ever even dreamt of thinking of. It seemed to be half a mile long with plenty of legs and great staring eyes. It moved like an underground railway train but much more slowly. It climbed over trees without bothering to notice them. It turned and made its way along the shore of the lake towards the people who were there waiting to see it. But they didn't seem to notice it. Perhaps they were looking the wrong way. The monster was creeping up behind them! Oh dear, it would eat them!

The Professor hurriedly pushed his way past all the stuff in the attic and leapt downstairs shouting, 'Quick! Quick! Monster on shores of lake! May eat people! Must warn them! Hurry, hurry!'

He shot out of his house just as Colonel Dedshott arrived on his horse to say *he* didn't believe all this stuff about monsters, by Jove. But the Professor clambered up beside him and gasped, 'To the lake! Monster at large! Rescue!'

The Colonel, who was never a one to ask the reason why, but only too ready to do and let's hope not die, spurred his horse on and arrived at the lake without the Professor, who had fallen off into a nice soft bush because he didn't go in much for horse riding.

But it was all right, after all, though more mystifying than ever. There was no monster on the shores of the lake and nobody there had seen anything, although most of them were all too eager to see something, never mind what, that might, with very elastic imagination, be thought to be a monster.

For what the Professor had seen out of the attic window was a caterpillar crawling along the glass. But the window was a bit murky and he had on the wrong spectacles for seeing things at a distance. And it looked to him as if some frightful monster was crawling along the shores of the lake, because from where he was the caterpillar on the window came just in the same place as the distant view of the lake edge.

'This is all very disturbing,' said the Mayor of Great Pagwell to some of the Councillors, over milk-shakes and jam tarts. 'Everybody thinks there is a monster and people are beginning to come from far and near and places in between to see it. But I don't think there is a monster.'

'Well, that's all right,' said the Councillor in charge of Zoos, who didn't particularly want to have to take in a monster who wouldn't fit into any of his nice cages. 'If there's no monster, why worry?'

'Tut, tut!' said the Mayor, stretching out his hand

for the last jam tart half a second after the Town Clerk
had taken it, 'it is not all right at all. These people are
coming to see our monster and there isn't one to see. It
will get us a bad name. People will say we spread a
rumour about a monster just to get people to come here.'

'Why don't we get Professor Branestawm to make us
a monster?' said one of the Councillors.

'A mechanical one,' cried the Town Clerk, 'that will
swim about and dive, and come up and be terrifying.'

'And yet quite harmless,' said the Zoo Councillor.

'Then Pagwell will become famous,' said the Town
Clerk. 'We shall have tourists. Business will buck up.
We can put the rates up.'

'Come on!' cried the Mayor, 'To Professor Branestawm's!'

'To the Professor's!' cried all the Councillors and
they dashed outside.

'The Mayor and Councillors to see you, sir,' said Mrs
Flittersnoop, opening the door of the Professor's study.
But she was instantly swept aside and nearly into the
waste-paper basket as the Mayor and Councillors
swarmed into the room.

'Well, really – er – gentlemen,' said the Professor
when they had managed to explain to him what they
wanted, which took a bit of doing because they kept
interrupting one another and adding things and contra-
dicting one another. 'Do I understand that you wish
me to – ah – invent a steam dinosaur, or diesel electric
sea serpent, or something of the kind?'

'Yes, rather!' shouted the Councillors.

'Ah – um – er,' muttered the Professor. 'You are not
afraid of – – er – inconvenient consequences?' he asked.
'I – er – mean to say, my inventions have sometimes

been known to become somewhat disordered through not being operated in the correct manner,' he said, 'and there has been trouble as a result.'

'Oh, no fear of that this time,' said the Mayor heartily, 'We only want the one monster and it will be kept in the middle of Pagwell Lake. Nobody allowed near it. I don't see that it can give any trouble.'

'Very well,' said the Professor, who thought it was going to be enormous fun inventing a monster, but wasn't going to say so in case he looked too eager, and Professors aren't supposed to be eager. It isn't dignified. 'I will make you a monster,' he said, 'on the condition that nobody is allowed to touch it. It must be for display only.'

'Done!' said the Mayor. 'But it must, of course, be kept the most deadly secret,' he added.

The Professor had a bit of a time of it, inventing the Pagwell Monster. To start with, as it had to be kept ferociously secret, he couldn't invent it in his inventory, where people might see it or get to know about it. So he decided to do his monster-making up in the attic. And of course, he couldn't tell Mrs Flittersnoop about it in case, by accident, she let slip a hint to her sister Aggie, who would then have had it all over the Pagwells in about two and a half seconds.

'Dear dear, this is most inconvenient,' muttered the Professor, scraping piles of old magazines and newspapers out of the way to make room for the monster-inventing.

But at last he got things a bit organized. He managed to smuggle inventing tools from his inventory up into the attic by telling Mrs Flittersnoop he was repairing the roof from the inside, which she thought funny but was used to the Professor doing funny things. Then besides inventing the monster, he had to keep inventing excuses for being up in the attic and not in his inventory. But the attic had one advantage. It contained several outrageous things that the Professor found most useful for inventing into the monster. There was an old dress-maker's model, for instance, that had once belonged to Mrs Flittersnoop's great aunt Jessica and could be made to expand or contract by turning a knob on top.

'Just the thing to make the monster appear to be breathing,' chuckled the Professor, connecting it up to a little motor.

Then there was an enormous stuffed head of a Canadian Moose or North Bobbletonian Hackledorfer or something of that kind, which, with a few dabs of highly coloured paint, and the addition of some threatening feelers and a couple of pudding basins fixed on over the eyes, made a quite passably terrifying head.

'I can't think what the Professor can be up to,' said Mrs Flittersnoop to her sister Aggie over the ironing. 'He's been up there in the attic these days and more. Says he's repairing the roof but it's my belief he's got some secret machine thing on the go.'

'Well, I hopes as how it isn't anything dangerous,' said sister Aggie, giving a hand with a sheet. 'Knowing as what the Professor can be like at times.'

'Yes, indeed,' said Mrs Flittersnoop. 'Not that I mind what he's up to,' she added, 'but it does make it difficult with the cups of cocoa to be taken up there and him never remembering to bring the cups down, so that I've run through two teasets and now having to give him his cocoa in flower vases and jelly moulds, as

he'll never let me up in the attic there to fetch the dirty cups.'

'Well, I dare say it'll be all for the best,' said sister Aggie, and they settled down to a cup of tea or two in wine glasses and some nice friendly gossip while the Professor went on happily monster-inventing overhead.

At last the monster was finished. The Professor had had to make it in sections because the attic wasn't big enough to take it all in one lump. Then there was some considerably hushed-up whispering kind of talk in the Mayor's Parlour at the Town Hall, to arrange about getting the monster taken down to the lake without any-body knowing about it.

'It must be done at night,' said the Mayor. 'Then nobody will see it.'

'What about the police?' asked the Town Clerk. 'They're sure to see it and may think we're burglars. Then we'll be arrested and the cat will be out of the bag, the monster will be in the soup and we shall very likely be in our own prison.'

'Wait a minute,' said the Mayor. 'Why can't we pretend we've got some municipal works going on to dredge the lake or something? Then people will think we're taking a dredger there.'

'We could take the monster there in bits and nobody would know what it was,' said the Town Clerk.

So the great monster-removing exercise was carefully planned and bit by bit the monster was taken down to the lake in fairly broad daylight, disguised as assorted municipal works, with the Councillors disguised in old clothes and cloth caps and false whiskers so as to look like municipal workmen.

At last the Professor's monster was fitted up and carefully lowered into the middle of the lake and right down to the bottom with no awkwardnesses except when the Mayor and two Councillors fell out of a little boat and had to be fished out on bamboo poles but as they were wearing old clothes no harm was done except to their municipal dignity.

'I have arranged to control the monster by radio electronic control,' said the Professor. 'From my attic,' he added. 'Pray stay there while I go home and give you a demonstration.'

He went back and climbed into the attic, carefully

avoiding Mrs Flittersnoop and a soup tureen full of cocoa and began to manipulate levers, wheels and switches.

Presently bubbles began to pop up on the lake. The water swirled. *Glug, glug, glug.* The monster rose gracefully out of the water, upside down and tail first.

'Coo!' muttered the Councillors.

'Er, um, sorry,' said the Professor, up in the attic where they couldn't hear him. He revolved wheels, pushed levers and adjusted thingummies.

The monster slid back into the water again. More glugging and bubbling took place. Five old boots, half a wooden wheelbarrow covered in green slime, and part of a motor car full of rust and water spiders rose to the surface, but were instantly pushed out of the way by the monster's head, which came up beautifully monster-like, followed by loops of body, and the whole lot went swimming gracefully round the lake.

'Wonderful!' cried the Mayor.

'Amazing!' cried the Councillors.

The monster emitted a puff of red smoke, snorted like a tugboat from Pagwell Canal and dived under the surface again, only to reappear further along, blowing fancy fountains all over the place.

'Bravo!' cried the Councillors, and they all swarmed up to the Professor's to congratulate him.

Come and see the Pagwell Monster! shouted posters in large, loud letters. *Only one of its kind! Terrifying! Ferocious! Appalling! No danger whatever! Admission free, children half price.*

Soon you couldn't see the shores of Pagwell Lake for people crowding to see the monster.

All the schools had special parties. Dr Mumpzan-meazle sent his patients to see it, feeling that a little imitation scarey might be good for their pains. The Vicar came and made up shattering sermons on the monsters that are after us in our everyday lives. Miss Frenzie of the Pagwell Publishing Company, who had hurt her foot when she fell over a plough at a farm she was staying at, came in a wheel chair. It was towed by her secretary, Violet, on a rowdy motor cycle with advertisements on it that said, *Read any Pagwell Paper-backs lately?* and *Pagwell Paperbacks are Spiffing.*

Up in his attic, Professor Branestawm put the monster through its paces time after time. He made it dive and rise, swim round in circles emitting barks and roars and puffs of smoke. He made it writhe and wriggle and lash its tail, and as it was nearly all tail the lashing was considerable.

Then what must happen, just as everything was going swimmingly, but Commander Hardaport (Retired) came seething down the lake in a little yacht.

'Avast there!' he cried, when he saw the monster puffing out smoke. 'Steam gives way to sail. Get out of my way there.'

But, of course, Professor Branestawm, up in the attic with levers and cups of cocoa, couldn't hear him. So the monster kept on a collision course, straight for the Commander, who used up all the nautical expressions he knew, then swerved away at the last split second to avoid hitting the monster, as he didn't want to damage the nice new paint on his nice new yacht.

'Lake-lubber!' he shouted as he shot by. And he walloped the monster's head a ninepenny one with a boat hook.

Well of course, you couldn't expect a Branestawm invention to stand being hit with boat hooks without doing something about it. The monster sloshed its tail round and batted Commander Hardaport (Retired) and his little yacht half way to the other end of the lake. Then it surged after him, blowing out red smoke and green flame trimmed with fancy stars.

'Good gracious!' cried the Professor, up in the attic, pulling levers. 'I fear the monster is getting a little out of hand. Why can't that fellow keep his yacht out of it?' He spun wheels, he operated switches.

Commander Hardaport (Retired) went about, and came shrieking down on the monster with his spinnaker flapping. But ha! The monster submerged, came up under the yacht and tipped it over, then retired to the other end of the lake, just as Colonel Dedshott, answering the Professor's call for help, arrived with a detachment of Catapult Cavaliers and a catamaran.

'After him!' shouted the Colonel. 'To the rescue!'

The Catapult Cavaliers paddled like mad and the catamaran shot across the lake at the double.

But they didn't make for the monster to beat it off. They made for the Commander.

'Get off the lake, by Jove!' shouted the Colonel. 'Leave that monster alone!'

The Commander got his yacht right way up, climbed in and set sail for the Colonel, waving the boat hook.

'Whose side are you on, hey?' he shouted, going red, blue and purple in the face. 'Monster attacked me! Took defensive action. Get after it. It's a public menace.'

There was just going to be the very wow of a naval and military battle when the monster came puffing up the lake blowing out smoke and stars. Colonel Dedshott and the Commander made hurriedly for the bank, where plenty of policemen got them ashore, while the monster went gliding round the lake, barking and roaring and bowing its head to the applause of the crowd.

'I feel it was somewhat unusual,' said the Professor afterwards, having tea with Colonel Dedshott, 'getting you to – ah – save one of my inventions from being attacked by someone, instead of the other way round.'

'Ha, my word, yes!' grunted the Colonel. 'Monster all under control, then?'

'Absolutely, my dear Dedshott,' said the Professor sadly. 'No trouble at all. But alas, it doesn't matter now. Everybody has realized that it is only a machine and not a real, live, meat-and-vegetables monster.'

'Yes,' said the Colonel. 'But you know, people are even more excited about it now they know it's a *Branestawm* invention. They're asking for future performances. Monster will have to appear every day. Only we can't have you stuck up in the attic working it, by Jove.'

'No, no, indeed,' said the Professor. 'Aha! I have it.' He waved his hands.

'Good,' snorted the Colonel, drinking his tea before the Professor could knock it over. 'What?'

'Automatic coin-operated monster-working meters,' said the Professor. 'The public gain admission to the lake by inserting coins in the meters placed there for the purpose. When sufficient coins have been inserted to make it worthwhile for the monster to perform, an electronic device actuates the monster which then goes through a twenty minute routine, after which the meters switch it off. I do not have to be in here, or – er – up there.' He pointed up to the attic.

'Wonderful!' cried the Colonel.

And sure enough, the Pagwell Monster went on delighting crowds, at ten pence a time, half price for children, with the automatic meters in full control, leaving the Professor free to concentrate on seventeen other inventions he had just thought of.

9

The Great Branestawm Take-Over

Chug, chug, chug, poppety, pop, zim zim. Professor Branestawm was driving happily along, keeping to the proper
side of the road, giving all the right signals, stopping at
all the pedestrian crossings, whether there were pedes-
trians desirous of crossing or not, and refraining from
overtaking other vehicles when it was not safe to do so.

'Um ah, ha,' he said to himself, 'most enjoyable. I'm
glad I decided to drive to Upper Snorkington to lecture
to the Society for the Promotion of Interesting Lectures
instead of going by train. So much simpler. None of
those tickets to get and no changing at so-and-so
junction with the possibility of getting on the wrong
train.'

Then he remembered he had forgotten the way to
Upper Snorkington, which wouldn't have mattered if
he had gone by train as engine drivers always know the
way, and even if they don't the lines take them there
anyway.

'Oh dear,' he said to himself. 'I had better ask the
way.'

Fortunately there was a nice large policeman standing beside the road, seeing that nobody stole the lamp-
posts. So the Professor drew up carefully beside him,
and said, 'Ah, um, excuse me, officer, can you direct me
to Upper Snorkington?'

'Yes sir, pleasure sir,' said the policeman, who

hadn't had anyone stop and ask him the way for ages, and meant to make the most of it. 'Just go along here until you come to the roundabout. Go right round the roundabout and take the third exit on the left.'

'But I thought one had to go left round a roundabout, not right round it,' said the Professor, being frightfully anxious to get everything clear.

'Yes sir, that's right. You go left round the roundabout but go right round it. Or at least go almost right round it and then go left.'

'But I cannot go right round it if I go left round it,' said the Professor.

Just then the policeman caught sight of a lady with a very large dog and he thought it would be a good excuse for getting away from the Professor if he asked the lady if she had a licence for her dog. So he said, 'You just follow the roundabout as I said, sir,' and strode off to speak to the dog lady.

'Oh dear,' said the Professor, 'I shall never understand this motoring business.' He started his car again, and soon arrived at the roundabout.

'I go left round the roundabout,' said the Professor to himself, going left round it after waiting for two red buses, a green bus and three enormous trucks to go left round it first. 'Then I go right round it.' Presently he came to a road leading off the roundabout that said *Great Pagwell.*

'Ha!' said the Professor. 'That's where I live. Now I know where I am.' And he shot off *chugetty, pop,* along the road to Great Pagwell, which, of course, was the road he had just come along, because he had gone right round the roundabout. Then he forgot he was supposed to be going to Upper Snorkington, missed the way back

to Great Pagwell, and eventually arrived at Twiddlebury Magna, where he had never been before, didn't
know anybody and nobody knew him.

At the market square of Twiddlebury Magna, five
roads meet, which makes it a definitely un-square
square. But it was certainly very much of a market
because it was simply littered with stalls of all kinds.

'Now let me see,' he said to himself, getting out of the
car and walking over to a greengrocery stall. He was
just looking at the oranges when the greengrocer man
said, 'Excuse me, sir, you have a kind face. Would you
mind just looking after my stall while I run home for a
bite of tea?'

'I – er – what did you – er, ah?' stuttered the
Professor.

'Thank you so much,' said the greengrocer. 'The
oranges are three new pence each, the apples are ten
new pence a pound, the grapes twenty new pence a
pound, and the asparagus is usually thirty new pence a
bundle but there isn't any today.'

'Dear, dear!' exclaimed the Professor. 'This is most
outrageous. I shall certainly not look after his – um –
greengrocery stall while he has any bites of anything.'

'Half pound of apples and four oranges, please,' said
a voice.

'How much are your grapes?' asked another voice.

'Give me two bananas,' said a third.

Three very large round ladies with feathers in their
hats stood in front of the stall.

The Professor, who had forgotten half of what the
greengrocer had said and hadn't listened to the other
half, thought he had better get rid of the ladies but got
himself most fantastically muddled up. He sold the first

lady half a pound of ten pence a pound apples for two pence. He tried to charge the second large lady ten pence a bunch for four oranges, but she took six and went away without paying anything.

A heavy hand dropped on the Professor's shoulder. He turned round and found himself looking at a very lofty policeman.

'Oh good gracious, dear me!' he thought. 'Now I suppose I shall be arrested for not being a proper green-grocer and not having a licence to greengroce.'

But he wasn't going to be anything of the kind. Later on he was going to wish he had been arrested and shut up in a nice little cell with nothing to do but invent new inventions. But he wasn't.

'Just give an eye to the traffic while I pop along and get my hair cut, there's a good chap,' said the police-man, taking off his helmet to show how much his hair needed cutting.

'But I – er, look here I – um – ah . . .' stuttered the Professor, clutching at spectacles as drowning men are supposed to clutch at straws, if there are any floating about.

'It's quite simple,' said the policeman. 'When you hold up your hand the motors and things will stop until you put your hand down. Now let the traffic go up High Street for a bit, then stop it and let George Street have a go, then give Victoria Parade a chance.'

'But you don't understand,' cried the Professor, beginning to hop up and down, 'I'm not, er, that is to say, I don't . . .'

'Two oranges and a nice hearty cabbage,' said a small thin lady.

'After which,' went on the policeman, taking no

notice of anything, 'turn 'em up the Avenue for a while, then swing over to Church Street. Then you start all over again. But don't forget, if you hear the fire engine, which isn't likely as the firemen are at a picnic, you must stop everything and clear the way.' He clapped his helmet on Professor Branestawm's head, and off he went.

'This is terrible!' groaned the Professor. 'How I wish Colonel Dedshott were here. He would know how to handle traffic. He's used to shouting out commands and making people left turn and right wheel and all that military sort of stuff.'

But what was the Professor to do? There was the traffic going most whizzily by and there was absolutely no policeman to control it, and there absolutely was the policeman's official traffic-directing helmet on the Professor's head.

He held up his hand to stop the traffic from going up anywhere but up George Street, just as the policeman had told him. But there was no traffic at that moment going anywhere but down George Street. A bright yellow motor car came zizzing into the market square.

'How much are these cauliflowers?' called a voice from the greengrocer's stall.

The Professor put his hand down and turned round. Instantly a bright blue van came out of Victoria Parade and ran smack wallop into the bright yellow car.

'Which is the way to the station?' asked an old lady, who had come up behind the Professor.

The blue and yellow motor drivers began arguing about whose fault the wallop was.

A bright red motor bus shot out of High Street and landed, *crash*, on the blue van and the yellow car.

'Help!' cried the Professor, getting half way to the greengrocery stall and trying to send three determined cyclists up the Avenue when they intended to go up Church Street.

'Finish sweeping this bit of road while I pop round the corner for a bit of cheese for supper,' said a road-sweeping man, pushing a broom into the Professor's hand.

'No, no, no!' shrieked the Professor.

'Thanks awfully,' said the road sweeper, disappearing in the direction of a cheese shop.

Professor Branestawm rushed madly across the market square sweeping up dust and leaves in a shower as he went.

A laundry man asked him to deliver a parcel while he saw to his white and gold laundry van which had just arrived among the muddle of traffic in the square.

The Professor dropped the broom and tore back to have a shot at weighing up seven pounds of potatoes.

'Mind my stall while I pop round the corner,' said the shrimp stall man, popping round the corner.

A bill poster kind of man plunked a pail of paste and a poster for somebody's toothpaste down on the Professor's toe and said, 'Be a good chap and paste this up over there for me. I want to catch my Auntie at the Post Office before it closes.'

The Professor looked frantically round for the somewhere to stick the toothpaste poster.

'Mind my doggie while I go to the library,' said a little girl, giving the Professor a string with a barking something on the end of it.

The three determined cyclists came spinning down Church Street, missed the collapsed traffic by inches and sent the shrimp stall flying in all directions.

'Oh, why didn't I stay at home? Oh, oh, oh, dear, dear!' squealed the Professor, sticking half the toothpaste poster on the back of a statue of the Mayor of Twiddlebury Magna, and giving the other half to the wrong person in mistake for the laundry, while the dog broke loose from the string, drank the rest of the paste from the bucket and went into the library after the little girl, which was drastically against all the rules.

Professor Branestawm was nearly in bits. He felt as if he had faces all round his head through trying to look everywhere at once, and arms and legs all over himself through trying to do everything at once, and no end of legs in bunches through trying to be everywhere at once or even sooner.

The greengrocer man had either been having a most unreasonably long bite of tea or else no end of many little bites. The policeman was either having all his hair cut right off a little at a time, or else getting the barber to make his eye-lashes look pretty. The crossing-sweeper who had popped round the corner for cheese, was either very difficult to please where cheese was concerned, or else he was very slow at popping – probably both. The bill poster man had either taken his Post Office Auntie to the pictures, or else was trying to buy a stamp at the telegrams counter, which is impossible, and the little girl in the library was most certainly having a day of it among the comic papers.

Just then, three large gentlemen in shirt sleeves bore down on him.

'I refuse to look after anything while anyone pops anywhere,' chattered the Professor.

'Ha, ha, ha! Jolly good, sir,' said the largest of the men. 'Well, I must say you did it even better than usual, which is saying a lot.'

'What?' squeaked the Professor.

'Easily the best picture we've done yet,' said the second shirt-sleeved man.

'A scream,' assented the third, looking very miserable.

'What *do* you mean?' cried the Professor. 'Have the goodness to – um – ah – stop it at once. I am Professor Branestawm of Great Pagwell.'

'Aw, come off it, Johnnie,' said the shirt sleeve number one. 'We know you've been playing an absent-minded Professor, and very well you've done it, but you can come out of your part now and be yourself.'

'My name is not Johnnie,' said the Professor, shaking spectacles at the three men. 'How dare you?'

The three shirt-sleeve men looked at each other. Their faces wriggled. Their eyebrows went up and down.

'Are you trying to tell us you *aren't* Johnnie Joyboy, the film star?' they said, grinding their teeth and looking sideways at him.

Just then who should arrive but Dr Mumpzanmeazle. He had been to a far distant hospital about a patient of his who wanted to go into Pagwell Hospital to have his toes straightened.

'Whatever is the matter, my dear Professor?' he asked, taking the policeman's helmet off the Professor's head and feeling his pulse.

'Here, who are you?' demanded the shirt-sleeve men.

'I rather think I should ask who you are?' said Dr Mumpzanmeazle. 'You are upsetting my friend Professor Branestawm, who appears to be in a very nervous condition and in need of treatment.'

The shirt-sleeve men clapped their hands to their foreheads and felt in need of treatment themselves.

At that moment up shot a very dusty someone on a most secondhand bicycle.

'Missed you, puff, puff, at the, puff, studio,' panted the someone. 'Rushed here, puff, puff, fast as could. Puff, telegram, urgent, puff.'

The largest shirt-sleeve man tore open the telegram.

'Sensational Film Productions,' he read out. 'Sorry but have pain in tum so do not feel like acting in comic film today Johnnie Joyboy.'

'Do you mean to say,' spluttered the Professor, while Dr Mumpzanmeazle tried to give him a calming-down pill, 'do you mean to say I have been doing all this for some film?'

'You certainly have,' said shirt sleeve, 'and some film it's really going to be, I'll say. You did it even better than Johnnie.'

'But that's ridiculous,' protested Dr Mumpzan-meazle. 'Professor Branestawm is not an actor. How could he possibly do it better than your film star?'

'Well,' said the big shirt sleeve, scratching his ear. 'I reckon it must be because he didn't know he was doing it.'

'How could I do something better because I didn't know I was doing it?' demanded the Professor.

Dr Mumpzanmeazle thought it all too likely that this could happen, but wasn't going to say so.

'Well,' said shirt sleeve, 'you see, you didn't know you were in a film so you just acted naturally as an absent-minded Professor would act.'

'Who says I'm absent-minded?' said the Professor, putting his spectacles on upside-down.

Nobody had an answer to this so the shirt-sleeve man went on, 'Johnnie Joyboy was supposed to act the part of an absent-minded Professor caught up in just the situation you were caught up in. If you had been asked to act the part you couldn't have done it, not being an actor. But as you didn't know it was a film you were just yourself and everything was fine.'

'Er, er, um,' said the Professor, who didn't feel at all himself.

'We thought you were Johnnie Joyboy because you looked exactly like Johnnie Joyboy when we rehearsed.'

And no wonder. Because Johnnie Joyboy had got his idea of an absent-minded professor from a picture of Professor Branestawm in the Pagwell Gazette.

Then they tried to talk the Professor into acting for more films. But although the Professor was quite willing to appear in a film about some learned subject such as the development of new environment-resistant species of seven-legged spiders, he certainly wasn't going to do any comic stuff for them or anyone else.

'But we shall send you some money for your help, Professor,' said shirt sleeves.

'Oh dear, no, not at all,' protested the Professor, who was horrified at the idea of being paid for something he didn't mean to do.

'But yes, we insist, my dear Professor,' said shirt sleeves. 'Our film will be an even bigger success than we hoped. It's only right that you should be paid for your services.'

'Oh well,' said the Professor, suddenly having ideas of exciting inventing tools he could buy with the money. 'If you say so.'

'Good,' said shirt sleeves. 'We'll post you a cheque and let you know where the film will be shown.'

'Ah, please do,' said the Professor. 'I am most anxious to avoid seeing it.'

'And after this distressing experience,' said the Professor, when Dr Mumpzanmeazle had got him home and Mrs Flittersnoop had got them both a very superior tea, 'I shall also avoid wherever possible all green-grocery stalls, road sweepers, laundry men, bill posters and little girls with dogs.'

10

The Grand Pagwell Regatta

COMMANDER HARDAPORT (RETIRED) leant on the fence and looked over into Professor Branestawm's garden as if he were leaning on the rail of a ship. And he spoke to Professor Branestawm rather as if he were shouting across to someone on another ship instead of to a gentleman standing by his geraniums three feet away.

'I say, we should have a Regatta, Professor,' he declared.

'A Regatta Professor?' said Professor Branestawm, looking puzzled through all five pairs of spectacles at once. 'I don't think there is such a person. Professor of Economics, yes; Professor of Music I suppose. But Professor of Regattas, er – um – ah, I don't think the Universities would approve.'

'I don't mean a Regatta Professor,' shouted the Commander. 'I mean we should have a Regatta. I only said Professor meaning you.'

'Dear me,' said Professor Branestawm. 'I fear I should not make a very good Regatta Professor. I have no knowledge of regattas.'

'No, *no*,' shouted the Commander. 'A Regatta. Races for yachts and boats and all that sort of thing, y'know. We should have one.'

'Ah, yes,' said the Professor. 'On Pagwell Canal perhaps. We have a yacht basin there, which I, er, arranged,' he said.

'Pah, no, not there!' snorted the Commander. 'Not that old ditch. Blue water, sir, that's what we want. But we're too far from the sea. How about the River Pag?'

'That would mean holding it at Pagwell-on-Pag,' said the Professor, 'and the Great Pagwell Council has no authority there.'

'Then we'll see the Pagwell-on-Pag Council,' cried the Commander. 'Come on, Professor. No time like the present.'

He clapped his hat on, grabbed his telescope, which he never went anywhere without, just in case, dashed into his garage, and emerged with blue smoke and considerable noises in a car that looked as if it ought to have guns and torpedo tubes on it.

'Ah, now,' said the Mayor of Pagwell-on-Pag, when the Commander told him of his idea. 'We have often thought a Regatta would be a nice attraction but unfortunately we do not have sufficient people to make it worth while.'

'I am sure,' put in Professor Branestawm, 'that the Great Pagwell Council would co-operate with you.'

'We could have a combined Grand Regatta of all the Pagwells,' said Commander Hardaport, dropping his telescope with a thud and picking it up again without one.

'Ah, now,' said the Mayor, who always seemed to start like that, 'perhaps we could arrange a meeting with the Great Pagwell Council.'

So the two Mayors and all the Councillors and various other people who were determined to be there in case it made them look important, were gathered together. It took a bit of doing because they all seemed to have foundation-stone-laying engagements or drains meetings, or conferences about roads and byeways, or discussions on parks and gardens, or tea parties in aid of needy grocers or visits to school sports.

Then there was a bit of a problem about where they should meet. If they had met at Great Pagwell Town Hall, the Pagwell-on-Pag Council would have felt a bit snubbed. And if they had gone to Pagwell-on-Pag Town Hall, the Great Pagwell Council would have objected. So at last all these vital people were gathered up and pushed politely into a nice neutral hall that belonged to the Salvation Army, and was nowhere in particular, and didn't offend anybody.

'We must have sculling and rowing races,' said Commander Hardaport, who did most of the arranging because he was the only one who knew the difference between those two things and the only one who knew anything about boats except that they are supposed to float. 'And, of course, yacht races,' he went on, 'but we need some unusual event to attract the crowds.'

'Climbing the greasy pole,' suggested a Great Pagwell Councillor.

'More suitable for a swimming gala,' snapped the Commander.

'Water history of the Pagwells,' said a Pagwell-on-Pag Councillor.

'Pageant, not Regatta,' snorted the Commander.

'Ah, now,' said the Mayor of Pagwell-on-Pag, 'I think it would be nice to have a beauty contest for a Regatta Queen, with handsome prizes.' He had several handsome daughters whom he thought might have a good chance of winning the prizes.

'Distraction!' cried the Commander. 'We'll have

plenty of shipshape little craft for the people to watch
without all those girls cluttering up the view.'

'Er, um, ah,' said Professor Branestawm, looking
over and under his pairs of spectacles. 'Might I suggest
a race for unusual vessels of original design.'

'Good idea!' said Commander Hardaport, wondering whether he could possibly borrow a torpedo boat
from the Navy to compete in. 'A free-for-all, y'know.
Any kind of boat, ship, vessel or craft of not more than a
certain size, to be propelled by any means the compe-
titors choose and first one home wins.'

'Ah, now,' said the Mayor, 'I think we should have
to make some restrictions. We cannot have people
tearing along in speedboats, kicking up a lot of wash
and causing flooding.' The Mayor lived in a house
beside the river.

Finally the rules for the Various Vessels race were
drawn up. They were:

1 No boat is to be more than thirty feet long.
2 No kind of fuel is to be used for driving machinery to
  propel the boat.
3 At least part of the boat is to remain in the water. (This
  was in case Professor Branestawm invented an unlikely
  flying boat.)
4 The first boat whose bows pass the winning post wins.
5 The judges' decision is final and no correspondence will
  be entered into.

Professor Branestawm was at work in his inventory
on an outrageous boat for winning the race.

'The chief problem is, Dedshott,' he said to the
Colonel, who had come to have his head sent round and
round by the Professor's explanations, 'to devise some
kind of machinery to propel the boat which does not

need fuel. This, of course, rules out electric motors, petrol motors, diesel, gas, steam and other conventional forms of machinery.'

'Ha yes, by Jove,' agreed the Colonel.

'So we are compelled to use a motive power that does not depend on fuel,' said the Professor, shuffling his spectacles. 'Man power, I fear, would not be strong enough unless we had a great number of men rowing but in a boat thirty feet long there would not be sufficient room, so I propose to use horse power.'

'I say,' said the Colonel, 'that means engines and things, doesn't it, and they need fuel. Against the rules, you know. Can't do that, Branestawm.'

'Ah no, my dear Dedshott,' said the Professor, 'I fear you do not understand me.' This was quite likely as the Colonel nearly always didn't understand the Professor.

'The horse power I propose to use is supplied by a horse,' went on the Professor. 'In fact, the horse power I propose to use is *your* horse, my dear Dedshott.'

'Ha, I see,' cried the Colonel, a great light suddenly breaking over him like a wave of warm dry water. 'You mean, get him to pull the boat from the towpath, as they used to do with barges.'

'No, no, no!' cried the Professor, shaking his head so rapidly that spectacles flew in all directions. 'We can't do that. Haven't you seen the notices on the river bank, "No horses allowed on the towpath"? I propose to use your horse *inside* the boat.' He pointed to a large drum. 'This is a kind of treadmill. You will ride your horse inside it. As the horse gallops the drum will revolve, thus driving, through a series of specially contrived gears, two paddle wheels at the sides of the boat. My gears, I may add, Dedshott,' he said, 'will increase the power of your horse by something like twenty times, so we should get a good turn of speed from the boat.'

'By Jove!' breathed the Colonel. The idea of riding his horse inside a boat had never occurred to him and he didn't like it much. But for the Professor, and to help the Professor win the Various Vessels race for the honour of Great Pagwell, he would do it. Yes by Jove, he would do it, and viva Great Pagwell, and God Save the Queen and other loyal noises.

'There are of course some other devices of my own in this boat,' said the Professor, taking the Colonel round and pointing out this, and indicating that, and explaining the other. 'So altogether I think we have a fair chance of winning.'

The Colonel thought they also had a fair chance of having no end of a dangerous time. But he was prepared for that. Dangerous times to any old friend of the Professor were to be taken in one's stride.

The day of the Pagwell Regatta dawned nice and early. And fine. And sunny. And with a nice fresh yachtsman's breeze. Which was all a bit too good to be true, but there it was.

On the bank of the Pag river, just where the Regatta races were to start, there was most conveniently an astonishing building with a tall tower, known as 'The Anglers' Pagoda'. Dignified fishermen used to meet there and say prayers that they would catch a lot of fish; while some of them climbed up the tower with telescopes ready to shout if they saw any fish coming. But now it was a sort of mini-supermarket, run by two gentlemen, a lady and a cat. And they did an enormous trade with the Regatta spectators, who bought quantities of sandwiches and packets of cakes to eat, as regattas are apt to be a bit exhausting to watch; and they sold bottles and bottles of Pagwell Pop, which is a kind of lemonade-flavoured ginger beer, coloured purple.

The banks of the Pag river were thick with people from all the Pagwells, some waving Union Jacks, some waving flags with encouraging messages such as *Great Pagwell for ever* and *Up the Lower Pagwellians* and *Go it Pagwell Gardens*. Some were waving their hats and some were just waving.

The river was thick with extraordinary boats, except for a strip down the middle for the races. There were boats that looked as if they had blocks of flats built on them. There were boats with balconies and even boats with pulpits, which the Vicar thought very nice. All the boats flew as many flags as possible and one or two flew washing as well. And every now and then a steamer came sliding past, absolutely stuffed with people and with bands playing at both ends.

Presently it was time for the races to start.

'Clear the course!' cried the Mayor of Great Pagwell and the Mayor of Pagwell-on-Pag, both at once. 'Let the first race begin.'

Then with a great deal of firing of guns and waving of flags the races began. Maisie and Daisie, the Vicar's twin daughters, got the first win for Great Pagwell in the canoe race, in which they finished first and most of the other canoes finished in the water.

Pagwell-on-Pag Rowing Club carried off the next race and the one after, but Great Pagwell Sailing Club got an easy first for the yachts because they had Commander Hardaport (Retired) who did some very pretty work sitting out his yacht on the curves and going about and tacking and doing no end of yachting things, so that he was past the winning post before some of the others had really started.

So that made it dead level. Great Pagwell must win the Various Vessels race to get the Grand Regatta Cup. This was a handsome silver sort of vase presented by Lord Pagwell. And it had engraved on it the mysterious words, 'Best pair of heifers', because it was really a cattle show cup that some cows belonging to Lord Pagwell had won at a bygone agricultural show.

'Well, well, so it is up to you, Professor,' beamed the Vicar, feeling extra angelic as his twin daughters had won the canoe race. 'I trust you will uphold the honour of Great Pagwell.'

The boats began to line up for the Various Vessels race.

Commander Hardaport (Retired) had rigged five masts on a little rowing boat and had every kind of sail on it he could think of, which was a great many. There were skysails, and upper and lower topgallants fore, main and mizzen. There were royals and jibs and stay-sails and balloon spinnakers. And altogether it looked like a mini-mini version of the Victory, the Cutty Sark and the Spanish Armada all at once.

Maisie and Daisie, in saucy little sailor hats and short seafaring pants, were steering a craft rowed by all their joint boy friends. And to get them all in they had four racing skiffs tied together.

Pagwell-on-Pag had entered a sort of four storey galley rowed by four tiers of firemen, policemen and market gardeners. The P-on-P Sports Club had a little skinny boat towed by ten of their best swimmers, and

the P-on-P Canoe Club had, instead of a canoe, a very long thin punt simply stuffed with energetic gentlemen paddling like mad.

Bong! The two Mayors of Great Pagwell and Pagwell-on-Pag both let off the starting cannon at once.

Cheers went up. The boats shot off. Water splashed over the people in the front rows. Excitement began to reign, but fortunately the rain didn't.

'Go it, Branestawm!' shouted the Great Pagwellians.

Colonel Dedshott on his horse inside the Professor's boat rode as he had never ridden before and certainly hoped he wouldn't have to ride again. The treadmill drum spun round. The gears whizzed and clicked. The boat leapt through the water with the Professor hanging on to the wheel, trying not to steer into the bank and only just succeeding.

Commander Hardaport's five masted square rigger swept majestically along as far as Pagwell Bridge which scraped all his five masts off as he went under it and left him with what looked like a boatful of inferior washing and a lot of second-hand bean sticks. So Commander Hardaport (Retired) retired.

Maisie and Daisie's boy friends in their multiple skiff went whistling past the Pagwell-on-Pag four storey galley. The boat towed by swimmers was neck and nose with the Canoe Club's punt. But hurray! Professor Branestawm's horse power boat was in front.

Round the first bend in the river Maisie and Daisie's boat came apart, the different bits collided with one another and the River Pag Conservancy Tugboat had to fish everybody out on poles.

Now it was up to Professor Branestawm. The honour of Great Pagwell depended on him. Could he beat the three Pagwell-on-Pag boats?

Thrum, thrum, thrum. Colonel Dedshott's horse galloped, the gears whizzed, the Professor steered. They were still in front but the four storey galley was gaining on them.

Then the Professor steered his boat the wrong way round an island and went up a backwater. Oh disaster! The Pagwell-on-Pag boats drew ahead. But the swimmers towing the Sports Club boat got mixed up with the paddlers in the Canoe Club punt and were out of the race.

The Professor's boat shot out of the backwater and nearly collided with the four storey galley. The Professor swung the wheel over and shot round another island.

The Professor took out some sandwiches Mrs Flittersnoop had given him, and passed one to Colonel Dedshott but his horse ate it. Then a cloud of hungry ducks, who had seen the sandwiches, came whirring over and landed on the deck.

'Ha!' cried the Professor, seeing what he thought

was a chance to get more speed on, 'tell them to flap their wings.'

But Colonel Dedshott had his mouth full of a rather glutinous sandwich the Professor had passed him.

Then out they came into the wide river again.

'Ha, well ahead now,' cried the Professor, not seeing the four storey galley. Then suddenly he saw it, a long way back. 'We're winning, Dedshott!' he cried, excitedly. 'The winning post must be in sight.'

It certainly was in sight. Half a mile behind.

'Dedshott! Dedshott!' shouted the Professor, jumping up and down and steering to port and starboard both at once. 'We've passed the winning post! We've won! The other boat must have dropped out.'

But just then the four storey galley came round a bend, approaching the winning post.

The island the Professor had gone behind extended past the winning post, so he had passed it without passing it, so to speak.

'Turn round and go back, by Jove!' shouted the Colonel, reining in his horse and turning it round in the treadmill drum so as to make the boat go backwards.

'No, no!' squealed the Professor. 'Go forward! I'll steer round.'

And with a tremendous amount of galloping hooves and shouting of encouraging noises and turning of the wheel and nearly hitting the bank they got the Professor's boat round and went tearing along back to the winning post.

'Approaching post from wrong side, by Jove,' panted the Colonel, who by now began to feel he was doing the galloping as well as the horse.

'Never, puff, mind,' gasped the Professor.

The four storey galley was nearly at the winning post. Professor Branestawm's boat still had some way to go. The excitement was intense. The people on the bank nearly came apart trying to shout and wave encouragement to both boats. A puff of wind blew the galley a bit off course but still it came on *splash, splash, splash*. Only a few yards to go and the Professor's boat was much further away. The Professor couldn't win and anyway he was the wrong side of the winning post.

The suspense was unbearable. People felt as if their ears were spinning round. Then *bong*! A sudden noise from the Professor's boat and it broke in two!

Oh disaster, after all! The Professor's boat had broken up. It would sink.

But ha! No, it hadn't and it wouldn't. The Professor had another trick up his waist-coat. The *bong* was a special catapult he had got the idea for from the Catapult Cavaliers artillery. It shot the bows of his boat off right past the winning post before the galley could get there.

'Hurray!' shouted the Great Pagwell supporters.

'Boo!' shouted the Pagwell-on-Pag supporters. 'Disqualified! Cheat! Ya! ya!'

'Hrrrmph,' said Professor Branestawm, arranging his spectacles carefully in the right order and looking at the row of important gentlemen in front of him. 'You will permit me to say, gentlemen, that I have won the Variable Vessels race strictly according to the rules which you drew up.'

'Nonsense!' shouted the Mayor of Pagwell-on-Pag, forgetting to say 'Ah now' first, because he was so cross.

'Your boat broke in two and anyway, you came from the wrong side of the winning post.'

'There is nothing in the rules,' said the Professor, 'that says a competitor has to pass the winning post from one side or the other.' And of course there wasn't.

'And,' went on the Professor, 'the rules say the boat whose bows first pass the winning post is the winner. It says nothing about the rest of the boat. The bows of my boat did pass the winning post first, so I have won.'

There was a bit of uproar at that, but the Mayors and Councillors had to admit the Professor was right, so the Grand Regatta Cup was handed to the Professor, who took it proudly home and Mrs Flittersnoop kept it on the mantelpiece in the front room, filled with flowers.

11

Professor Branestawm in Orbit

OH, DREADFUL DISASTER! Oh, tearful tragedy! Oh, Pagwellian plight! Great Pagwell Town Hall was attacked by dry rot.

It was first discovered by the head Tea-Taker-Round bringing the Mayor's tea to the Mayor's Parlour when he vanished through the floor accompanied by clouds of smelly dust and the Mayor's own special private tea set, to say nothing of several slices of best Town Hall bread and butter, and a plate of municipal meringues.

· 'Fetch the Borough Surveyor!' cried the Mayor. 'I'm going to Penelope's Pantry for tea.'

'I'm sorry to say, Mr Mayor, your worship sir,' said the Borough Surveyor next day, 'that the entire Town Hall is riddled with dry rot. Steps will have to be taken to re-build the staircases. The ball-room floor is all room and no floor. The entire east side has gone west and the Council Chamber has gone to pot, er, so to speak.'

The Mayor clapped a hand to his head and leant against the wall, which crumbled up like cake crumbs and landed him in the middle of a very stuffy meeting of Air Conditioning Engineers that was going on in the next room.

'Call an emergency meeting of the entire Council,' he ordered. 'We must decide what action to take.'

The Council assembled in the Church Hall.

'Why don't we get Professor Branestawm to invent

something to deal with the rot?' asked a very young Councillor.

'But the rot has already dealt with the Town Hall,' said the Mayor. 'When we stop the rot we shall have to start building a new Town Hall.'

That instantly switched the meeting to the exciting and highly arguable subject of what the new Town Hall was to look like.

Some wanted it to look exactly like the old Town Hall, which would have been difficult because they had lost the recipe. Others wanted it to be frightfully modern, which might have been frightful. Some wanted it to be built entirely of black glass, while still others didn't want a Town Hall at all but a Municipal Complex, which would have meant knocking down the whole of Great Pagwell, West Pagwell, Pagwell Gardens and Upper Pagwell to make room for it. And as all the Councillors lived in one or other of those places the idea was heavily defeated.

'It is a pity they did not call me in earlier,' said Professor Branestawm, when he heard about things. 'I could no doubt have devised some, um, ah, means of dealing with the dry rot before it became undealable with.'

'Yes, indeed, I'm sure, sir,' said Mrs Flittersnoop. 'I always thought there was a funny smell about the Town Hall,' she went on, 'but I thought it was due to the way they cook their cabbage, sir, which does hang about so if you aren't careful. Not that I don't think cabbage is good for one, because you can't have too many greens, as I always say.'

'Um,' said the Professor, 'well, perhaps they will

ask my advice about some kind of treatment for the new Town Hall, to prevent any dry rot attacking the new edifice.'

'All the same, Branestawm,' cried Colonel Dedshott indignantly, 'I reckon they should have brought you into it. Respected citizen of long standing and all that. Notable record of achievements, by gad! Disgraceful to ignore you in this manner!'

'Letter for you, sir,' said Mrs Flittersnoop, coming in just then with a big envelope.

'Mrs Flittersnoop! Colonel Dedshott!' cried the Professor excitedly, waving the letter in one hand and bunches of spectacles in the other. 'Remarkable news! A great compliment. I really, am, um, ah, that is to say I never expected . . .'

'No indeed, I'm sure, sir,' said Mrs Flittersnoop, folding her hands and waiting patiently for the Professor to unscramble himself and say what he was talking about.

'The Mayor,' panted the Professor, 'and the Pagwell Council! They have done me the honour to ask me to . . . Here read it for yourselves.' He pushed his spectacles into Mrs Flittersnoop's hand and tried to put the letter on his nose.

'*Dear Professor Branestawm,*' said the letter,

We are planning a Grand Civic Opening for the new Town Hall, when completed and we were wondering whether you would care to provide some kind of device or diversion by way of public entertainment after the Ceremonial Lunch. We feel that as a public figure of such interest and respect you would be a fitting person to do this. Perhaps a special invention of some kind would be suitable.

'Well, I never, indeed, sir,' said Mrs Flittersnoop, coming all over delighted, 'not but what they should do something to make up for not asking you about the Town Hall in the first place.'

'But the question is, Dedshott,' said the Professor, when the Colonel had finished congratulating him, 'what shall I invent? What would be suitable for opening a new Town Hall?'

The Colonel's ideas about celebrating something usually ran to salutes of goodness knows how many guns and parades of rows and rows of soldiers all in their best clothes, marching up and down to the sound of very crashy military music and much roaring out of commands. But he knew better than to suggest that the Professor should invent a new and probably highly risky kind of saluting gun, or offer to lend him any Catapult Cavaliers to play with.

'Sounds as if they expect you to do some confounded conjuring tricks,' he grunted. "Device or diversion by way of public entertainment" it says.' He picked up the letter. 'What do they think you are, Branestawm, hey? High wire walker or something of the kind?'

'What did you say, Dedshott?' said the Professor. 'High wire walker?'

'Hrumph, only joke, m'dear fellow,' barked the Colonel.

'Yes, yes, of course,' said the Professor. 'But it gives me an idea. I have been working on a new invention to do with weightlessness. How to overcome it, you know. For those astronaut people exploring outer space.'

'Hrumph,' said the Colonel, exploring inner space with another biscuit.

'Now I have been experimenting with ideas to overcome weightlessness,' said the Professor. 'All I have to do is to reverse the process and what do we have?'

'No idea,' grunted the Colonel as his head started going round in its usual orbit when listening to the Professor's explanations.

'Why the reverse of overcoming weightlessness, if you already have it, is to create weightlessness if you do not have it, you understand?' said the Professor.

'Of course, precisely,' said the Colonel, not understanding anything.

'So,' went on the Professor, 'if I achieve weightlessness I can create a public sensation by walking high up in the air with no high wire or anything else to support me.'

'Wonderful, by Jove!' exclaimed the Colonel, who often went up in the air over the things his soldiers did on parade, but didn't need to be weightless to do it. 'But a bit risky, what? Suppose it doesn't work?' But the Professor was already off inventing.

Time went by. The Pagwell Council agreed to have a Town Hall of traditional design with fancy balconies, ornamental statues, beautiful balustrades and a magnificent tower. And to please the people who wanted it modern and contemporary there was to be an annexe, at the back where it wouldn't show too much. It was a very advanced kind of annexe made of black glass, with absolutely straight sides and no means of finding the front entrance. And the builders got to work and the place was littered with curious cranes and panting and puffing machinery, and dozens of little men with tin wheelbarrows and other men with sheets of paper fastened on to little boards, and heaps of building stuff wherever it would get most in the way, and notices saying *Keep out* and *No admittance* and *Road closed* and *Go away*.

And inside Professor Branestawm's inventory the air was thick with a thousand smells, most of them frightful. Coloured smoke went up from time to time. There were occasional bangs. Mrs Flittersnoop had a bag packed ready to leave for sister Aggie's at short notice if anything really drastic happened, but happily it never did.

'Success! Success!' shouted the Professor dashing out of his inventory. 'Branestawm's Weightlessness Inducer,' he cried holding up a bottle of red liquid.

'It smells like raspberry essence,' said Mrs Flittersnoop, sniffing gingerly at it.

'Yes, it tastes rather like it too,' said the Professor. He took a small tip, rose ten inches off the ground and went wafting and wobbling round to tell Colonel Dedshott.

Posters broke out all over the Pagwells.

Grand opening of the new Town Hall at Great Pagwell, they shouted, in violet letters on a violent pink background. *Civic Lunch in the new Council Chamber followed by a special demonstration of astronautical weightlessness by Professor Branestawm who will walk in mid-air from the tower of the new Town Hall to the Tower of Great Pagwell Church.*

'I hope he knows what he's doing,' said Dr Mumpzanmeazle, feeling a bit nervous for the Professor. He made a note to order a few ambulances just in case.

'There ought to be a safety net,' said the Councillor in charge of municipal tennis courts. 'I could soon rig one up with a few tennis nets.'

Eventually the grand opening day dawned loud and clear, with the sun shining and the Pagwell Town Band practising the ceremonial march specially composed for the occasion by their bandmaster, Mr Strongblow and called Pride of Pagwell, though Farmer Plownough said it sounded more like the name of a prize pig.

The new Town Hall was very nearly finished, apart from a few odd bits of scaffolding the builders hadn't been able to get undone, and one or two piles of sand. And the whole place was so done up in bunting and flags and gay garlands it all looked like a cross between a fun fair and a glorious road works.

In front of the Town Hall the Pagwellians were sitting on rows and rows of municipal seats and those who couldn't find room on the seats sat in semi-circles on piles of sand. Mrs Flittersnoop and her sister Aggie had a nice picnic basket on the back of Cousin Bert's lorry, with the vegetables pushed well up to the front to make room.

There were the mixed choirs of all the Pagwell schools ready to let fly with suitable hymns, led by the choir of Pagwell Church, conducted by the Vicar himself in his best surplice.

And inside the new Council Chamber were assembled the entire Pagwell Council, which had assembled very easily as there was a banquet to deal with instead of Council business, so they had all arranged not to be on holiday or ill in bed, or otherwise engaged. The Mayor was presiding, of course, and Colonel Dedshott was there, accompanied by General Shatterfortz and rows of other highly ornamental and important personages. In fact the only important person who wasn't there was Professor Branestawm, and he, of course, was behind the scenes, all ready for his great Weightless Walk.

'Well, rather you than me,' said the chef from Great

Pagwell Hotel, who was in the new Town Hall kitchen getting the banquet ready.

'There is no danger, I assure you,' said the Professor. He took out the bottle of Weightlessness Inducer and put it down on the table while he fixed his five pairs of spectacles on with sticky tape in case they should fall off and be bashed to pieces while he was up in the air.

Then he picked up the bottle and climbed up to the topmost top of the Town Hall tower.

Inside the Town Hall the banquet oozed to its finish.

'This custard is delicious, I must say,' said the Mayor. 'I must get the chef to give my wife the recipe.' He finished the custard and stood up.

'I rise to propose the health of Great Pagwell,' he said. And he rose all the way up to the ceiling.

'Er, um, ha!' said the Town Clerk, wondering if it had really happened or if he had had too much banquet.

Then the Chief of the Fire Brigade went up to join the Mayor.

The next moment up shot the Vicar, clutching frantically at the chandelier and looking, in his clean surplice, rather like an astonished angel.

Four Councillors shot up and hit the ceiling with slight bongs.

'Whatever are you thinking of?' cried the Town Clerk's wife. 'Such behaviour . . .' Then she went up too, but only half way, as she was rather on the stout side.

The Town Clerk scrambled down the wall like a spider, but shot up to the ceiling again as soon as he let go of the furniture.

Oh frightful situation! The banquet had finished with apple pie and raspberry flavoured custard. Professor

Branestawm had picked up the wrong bottle in the kitchen. The chef had made the custard with his Weightlessness Inducer. Tut, tut!

But goodness gracious, much worse than that. There was Professor Branestawm waiting on the topmost top of the Town Hall tower with what he thought was his bottle of Weightlessness Inducer. But it was really only raspberry essence. It wouldn't induce any weightlessness. He would crash to the ground!

In the Council Chamber the guests were still up in the air. The Mayoress was hovering perilously over the coffee cups.

'By Jove!' gasped Colonel Dedshott, who was still down on the floor as he didn't care much for custard – soldiers don't. Suddenly he saw, with his military penetration, what had happened. 'Branestawm by Jove!' he cried. 'Remember he told me his weightless stuff tasted of raspberry essence. Custard tastes of it too. Somehow he must have the wrong bottle. He'll crash to the ground. My word, what!'

Hurriedly he grabbed the custard bowl and gulped down plenty of spoonfuls. Then clutching at furniture and hanging on to anything in sight, he crawled out of the Council Chamber, down the grand corridor, and along bits of left-over scaffolding to the tower.

Bong, bong, bong, the clock in the tower struck three.

'Time for my weightless walk,' said Professor Branestawm. He took a drink of raspberry essence and stepped on to the parapet. Colonel Dedshott let go of everything and went sailing into the air. Professor Branestawm stepped off the tower and fell, *whiziziz,* like a queer-shaped stone.

Colonel Dedshott stretched out his hand and made a

grab at him as he went by. Ha! He caught the Professor's coat-tails. There was a frantic clutching and snatching and a sort of unlikely mid-air dance, and gradually a bunched-up mixture of Colonel and Professor floated gently to the ground.

'Oh ah, thank you, Dedshott,' panted the Professor. Then Colonel Dedshott explained what had happened. 'Dear, dear,' said the Professor, 'I must tell the Mayor at once! I must explain, yes indeed, I must.'

He rushed into the Town Hall.

'Professor Branestawm!' shouted the Mayor from the ceiling. 'What is this, some idiotic invention of yours or what? Get us down from here at once.'

'Er, um, ah yes, of course,' said the Professor. 'Fortunately I prepared an antidote to the weightlessness as I had no wish to remain permanently floating in space.' He took a little box out of his pocket. 'Have the goodness to take one of these tablets,' he said.

But of course there was a frightful business of trying to get the tablets up to the people on the ceiling.

'Tell Colonel Dedshott to shoot them up to us with his catapult,' cried the Mayor, having a bright idea.

'Colonel Dedshott!' cried the Professor, suddenly realizing things.

He rushed outside just in time to see a Colonel-shaped speck disappearing into the clouds. The moment the Professor let go of him, Colonel Dedshott had gone sailing up into the air! The Colonel would go on whizzing up and upper and upper. There was no ceiling to stop him. He would be lost in outer space!

'Fire tablets up to him, out of a cannon,' cried General Shatterfortz.

But Professor Branestawm had a nobler idea. Frantically he finished up the raspberry custard, grabbed the antidote tablets, tore outside and shot up into orbit after the Colonel.

'Oh dear, oh dearie me, I knew he shouldn't have done it,' wailed Mrs Flittersnoop. 'He'll never get down in time for dinner and he's had no proper lunch, even if he's eaten the sandwiches I gave him.'

Everywhere was uproar. Some of the people had been told what had happened. Others guessed and got it wrong, and the rest didn't know what was up but knew something was. Breaths were bated everywhere.

'They'll go into orbit for ever!' cried the Head-

master of Pagwell College. But suddenly shouts went up, without the aid of any raspberry custard.

'Look! Look!' shouted everyone.

A double speck appeared through the clouds. It was the Colonel and the Professor. They came sailing slowly down and made a perfect splash down in one of the new Town Hall fountains, though without any splash as the fountain wasn't working yet.

'Well, I must say you managed to give the new Town Hall a good send off, Professor,' said the Mayor, when things had been sorted out.

'Er, um, ah, yes,' said the Professor. 'And as a by-product of my Weightlessness Inducer I have created an entirely new substance with which the new Town Hall can be treated to make it proof against dry rot in the future.'

'Hope it stops some of the rot talked at Council Meetings too,' grunted the Mayor.

12

The Professor Remembers

IT WAS BOUND to happen eventually. It had been sort of threatening to happen several times. And now it actually positively had really happened.

Professor Branestawm had been awarded the Freedom of Great Pagwell.

Yes, rather. It was partly in honour of his having done a sensational and not altogether intended walk in space at the opening of the new Town Hall, partly for some of the other things he had done for Great Pagwell, mostly while trying to do something entirely different, and partly because he could then travel free on the buses and that would save the Pagwell bus conductors a lot of trouble, as he usually forgot to take any money with him. It would also save the Pagwell Councillors from having to answer letters he frequently wrote complaining he had been charged too much for being taken somewhere he didn't want to go. And anyway the Mayor wanted it because it meant a banquet and the Mayor loved banquets.

'When is the presentation taking place, what?' asked Colonel Dedshott, reckoning he must sweep up a nice large assortment of Catapult Cavaliers, in their best uniforms and their hair cut so short you could hardly see it, to form a guard of honour for the Professor.

'I er, that is to say, let me see,' said the Professor. 'I have it written down somewhere.' He fished various pieces of paper out of his pocket. Some of them were letters he had forgotten to post. Some were old bus tickets. Some were notes about new inventions, but none was the particular bit of paper on which he had written the date when he was to be made a Freeman of Great Pagwell.

'Dear, dear me, this will never do,' he said. 'If I am to be given the Freedom of Great Pagwell the least I can do is to be there, and how can I be there if I do not know the date? Tut, tut, it is most careless of the Pagwell Council not to have told me the date.'

Of course the Pagwell Council had told him the date. They had told him in a very ornamental letter with coloured capital letters and gold full stops, surrounded by coloured squirly bits and the arms of Great Pagwell. But the Professor had taken it to be framed because he thought it much too handsome-looking to be left lying about. And he had forgotten he had taken it to be framed and even if he had remembered he would have forgotten which shop he had taken it to.

'Disgraceful!' thundered the Colonel. 'I shall speak to them about it.'

He got on the telephone to the Town Clerk and said, 'When is Professor Branestawm being given the Freedom of Great Pagwell, that's what I want to know? When is he, answer me that, what, by Jove?'

The Town Clerk was so taken aback by this fierce demand, he thought the Colonel was complaining about the Professor not being given the Freedom.

'But my dear Colonel, the Professor *has* been given the Freedom of Great Pagwell,' he said.

'What's that?' roared the Colonel. 'You mean he has been given the Freedom and you never let him know the date so that he could be there?'

'No, no – er, that is, yes, yes,' spluttered the Town Clerk. 'The Professor has been awarded the Freedom of Great Pagwell, but the ceremony has not yet taken place.'

'That's what I'm asking you, confound you!' roared the Colonel, blowing his whiskers out straight and sending the pictures crooked on the wall. 'When's it to be, what?'

'The date of the ceremony,' said the Town Clerk, 'is the er, ah, er, let me see . . .' He ran his finger down the calendar past the Mayor's Birthday Party, across the League of Leisurely Bank Inspectors' Annual Picnic, over the Municipal May Day Celebrations and at last reached the date of dates. 'It will take place on February 29th precisely,' he said, and rang off quickly.

'February 29th,' said the Colonel to the Professor. 'The last day of next month. Should be easy to remember.'

'Ah yes, of course,' said the Professor. 'I had better write it down.' He had the most second-hand bargain sale sort of memory. He often forgot his meals and then wondered why he was hungry. He forgot where he lived but fortunately nearly everybody else knew so he had only to go up to someone and say, 'Excuse me, do you know where Professor Branestawm lives?' Then they would usually say, 'But you *are* Professor Branestawm, aren't you?' Then he would say, 'Tut, tut, I'm not asking you if you know Professor Branestawm, I'm asking you if you know where he lives.'

So the Professor wrote *Freedom of Pagwell, February 29th* on a piece of paper and put it behind the clock. Only it was the clock in Colonel Dedshott's house.

Next day the Vicar came round to enquire the date

of the Freedom-presenting so that he could arrange for suitable hymns for the Pagwell Ladies Choir to sing for the occasion.

'Er, um, oh dear dear,' said the Professor, 'now I made a special note of the date, but where did I put the note?'

Just then the clock struck one o'clock though it was really a quarter to eleven, but the Professor had been inventing the clock about a bit.

'Ha!' said the Professor. 'That's it! I remember I put a note behind the clock in Colonel Dedshott's sitting-room.' But alas, it wasn't there now. The Colonel's Catapult Cavaliers butlers had found it and thrown it carefully in the fire because it was making the room look untidy and their military minds simply couldn't stand a litter of rubbish all over the place.

'The date of the Presentation of the Freedom is February 29th,' said Professor Branestawm, when he had found out from Colonel Dedshott, who had found out from the Town Clerk again. He wrote it carefully on several bits of paper and put them under different parts of the carpet.

Two days later the tailor, who was going to make the Professor a special suit for being presented with the Freedom of Pagwell in, called to ask the date so as to have the suit ready in time.

Of course the Professor couldn't remember but Mrs Flittersnoop's cat came in just then with a little mouse which it pushed under the carpet.

'Ha!' cried the Professor, remembering where he had put his memory-jogging notes. But alas, there was nothing under the carpet, not even a speck of dust. Mrs Flittersnoop had been having a good clean-up after her sister Aggie's visit and she had swept up the bits of reminding paper, not knowing that was what they were, and thrown them away.

'Oh good gracious, tut tut!' cried the Professor. 'Am I never to be allowed to jog my own memory? I know I shall never remember the date of this Freedom-presenting business. And if I'm not there, goodness knows who they'll give the Freedom of Great Pagwell to. I shall be in the Town Clerk's bad books. I shall be in bad odour with the Drains Councillor and they'll charge me double on the buses.'

He managed to get hold of the date again and wrote it on his shirt cuff but Mrs Flittersnoop's washing-machine, that the Professor had invented for her, had stopped washing shirts, so she sent the Professor's shirt to the laundry and he was foiled again.

'This is really getting beyond a joke,' cried the Professor. He was so forgetful he had even forgotten it hadn't been a joke to start with.

Time after time he tried to remind himself of the important date. He wrote it in his library book but changed the book without thinking. He marked it on a calendar but it happened to be one Mrs Flittersnoop was sending to a distant cousin in Australia. He wrote it on the shopping list in the kitchen but Mrs Flittersnoop thought it was an invitation from the milkman to go to the pictures.

He inscribed it on the first page of a brand new exercise book he bought specially for it. But Miss Frenzie carried the book way along with a clutch of papers she had with her when she came to see the Professor. And when she found it, not knowing where a nice new exercise book came from she gave it to the

Headmaster of Lower Pagwell School. And the Professor's memory-jogging note was copied out thirty-five times in assorted kinds of handwriting, translated into three different languages, added up, divided and subtracted as an unexpected kind of sum and finally torn up and made into paper boats and disposed of in Pagwell Canal.

He wrote himself a letter to remind him of the date but forgot to stick the envelope down so the letter came out and the envelope arrived empty.

'Some people really are ridiculous,' he muttered, peering into the empty envelope to see if anything resembling a letter might be lurking in a corner. 'Fancy sending me an envelope when I already have plenty of them!'

He sent himself a postcard of Great Pagwell Town Hall with the date of the presentation written as enormously as possible on both sides. But he forgot to put his address on it, so it went severely astray and finished up in the lost letter office, folded up small to stop the Head-lost-letter-looker-for's window from rattling.

'Dear, dear, this is most unreasonable,' the Professor grunted. 'It is unbearable.'

He put a note in his hat but it blew away the first time he raised his hat to a lady. He tried to tie twenty-nine knots in his handkerchief but had to give up at the ninth and found it very knobbly for blowing his nose on. He actually managed to cut twenty-nine notches in his walking stick, but it fell to bits as soon as he had finished.

Then all of a sudden he found that everything was all right. He had been writing the date of the Presentation of the Freedom of Great Pagwell so many times he found he could actually remember it.

'Great news, Dedshott!' he cried, tearing round to the Colonel's with his spectacles flying in all directions. 'I can remember the date of the Presentation at last! It is to be on the twenty-ninth of this month.'

'Ha, hrrmph!' said Colonel Dedshott, 'jolly good, by Jove! But better check up, what?'

He took down from the wall a calendar covered in pictures of soldiers and studied it.

'By Jove, Branestawm, you've remembered it all wrong, you know,' he cried, pointing a finger at the calendar. 'It isn't the twenty-ninth of this month.'

'My dear Dedshott,' protested the Professor. 'It *must* be the twenty-ninth of this month. It is the only thing I have managed to remember so I ought to know.'

'This month is February,' cried the Colonel stabbing a finger at the calendar.

'Good gracious!' said the Professor, looking at the calendar through various combinations of pairs of spectacles. 'But there does not appear to be a twenty-ninth! February has only twenty-eight days.'

'Must be Leap Year,' grunted the Colonel.

But it wasn't Leap Year, and there wasn't a February 29th.

Oh dear, dear, and good gracious, the Town Clerk had been in such a state with the Colonel shouting at him that he had been looking at last year's calendar which he hadn't been able to bring himself to throw away because it had such a pretty picture on it.

'This is a fine state of affairs, I must say,' said the Professor, meaning of course that it wasn't a fine state of affairs at all. 'Here am I, going to be given the Freedom of Great Pagwell on a date that doesn't exist. What's to be done, Dedshott?'

'Ah hrmmph,' said the Colonel. 'I shall telephone the Town Clerk!'

'This is extremely inconvenient,' said the Mayor when he heard about things. 'If the Professor's Freedom can't be presented on February 29th, when can it be presented? February 28th?'

'Er, no, I fear that is the date of the Fire Brigade's annual display,' said the Town Clerk.

'Well, what about March 1st?' said the Mayor.

'That, alas, is booked for the Girls' Friendly Society's Dance and they would be furious if we altered it.'

'Then we must postpone it a few days,' said the Mayor.

But it turned out that the Town Hall and all the important Pagwell people were booked solid for months. There wasn't a day free to give the Professor the Freedom.

'All right,' said the Mayor, bringing his fist down thump on the table and causing the inkpot to jump up and give the Town Clerk a blue-black nose. 'I have decided. It is a momentous decision, but I have made it. We shall do something that has never been done before in the annals of Great Pagwell.'

'Um?' said the Town Clerk, who saw something awkward coming but couldn't see how to dodge it.

'Since there is no day free for the Freedom, ha, ha,' said the Mayor, pausing only to laugh at his own joke, 'we shall present the Freedom to the Professor at night.'

'What?' squealed the Town Clerk, going all of a shiver.

'At twelve o'clock midnight, precisely,' said the Mayor, 'with firework displays.'

'And torchlight processions,' added the Town Clerk, reckoning he had better sound a bit enthusiastic about it in case the Mayor thought of something even more drastic.

'Pagwell will go down in history as the first place to hold a Freedom Presentation at midnight,' said the Mayor, flinging out his hands and knocking no end of cups of tea off a tray someone was just bringing in. 'And we shall have done the calendar in the eye, so to speak,' he added, stepping back out of the spilled tea on to dry land and on to the Town Clerk's foot. 'By having the ceremony at midnight on February 28th we shall in effect be creating a February 29th that doesn't exist.'

'Bravo!' said the Town Clerk hurriedly, instead of a more explosive word he was going to say when the Mayor trod on his foot. 'I only hope there isn't a bye-law against it,' he added.

'To blazes with the bye-laws!' cried the Mayor magnificently and he swept out, kicking spilt cups of tea in all directions.

'Well indeed, I'm sure, sir,' said Mrs Flittersnoop when she heard about the arrangement, 'I do think that's clever, sort of slipping an extra day into the calendar specially for the Professor. And let's hope it's nice and sunny,' which, of course, was unlikely as it was going to be the middle of the night, but her intention was well meant.

So everything was fixed up for the grand midnight Presentation of the Freedom of Great Pagwell to

Professor Branestawm, by floodlight, accompanied by fireworks.

And Professor Branestawm made sure he would remember the date this time by asking Colonel Dedshott to call for him and take him along to the Town Hall. He also told Mrs Flittersnoop to remind him not to go to bed that night as he didn't want to receive the Freedom of Great Pagwell in his pyjamas.

The presenting ceremony itself was a huge success. Everybody ate too much, all the fireworks went off first time and none of the torches in the procession went out too soon. The Mayor presented a highly ornamental parchment scroll covered in coloured writing with gilded capital letters saying that the Professor was now a Freeman of Great Pagwell. And the scroll was in an elaborate and very choice casket. ('Just right for keeping the Professor's clean handkerchiefs in,' declared Mrs Flittersnoop.)

Professor Branestawm made a speech in which he

thanked the Mayor and Councillors and people of Great Pagwell for the honour. Then he went on to tell them some things about the motivating action of heredity on the habits of five-legged beetles in the western isles of Wow Wow. And a good time was had by one and all.

But whatever else he may forget, Professor Branestawm will always remember nearly forgetting to be present when he was presented with the Freedom of Great Pagwell. It was a great day, was that night.

About the Author

Norman Hunter writes: 'I was not invented by Professor Branestawm. I was born. In London, 1899, a few years after the other Normans got there. After escaping from school I had a course in all-in wrestling with typewriters and eventually inserted myself into the advertising profession. I wrote advertisements of such allure that people bought vast quantities of the most unlikely things before they could stop themselves. I am also a conjuror and managed to let off two hundred performances at Maskelyne and Devant's before the Nazis hit it with a bomb.'

Mr Hunter was in Johannesburg for twenty years, but has now returned to England and lives in a riverside cottage on the Thames where he continues to write Professor Branestawm adventures.

Also in Puffins: *The Incredible Adventures of Professor Branestawm, Professor Branestawm's Treasure Hunt, The Dribblesome Teapots and Other Stories, The Home-made Dragon and Other Stories, The Peculiar Triumph of Professor Branestawm, Professor Branestawm's Dictionary,* and *The Puffin Book of Magic.*

Jennifer, Hecate, Macbeth and Me

E. L. KONIGSBURG

This is a deliciously macabre, deliciously comical story of Elizabeth's fascinating friendship with Jennifer the witch, the girl who could produce watermelons in January and toads in frozen March, and walk round corners and up and down curbs without ever looking down. As an apprentice witch she endured months of special diets, of charms and incantations, of investing all their bicycling time, cinema time, roller-skating time and lounging-around-the-house time in their magical studies, until April came and it was time to try the flying spell . . .

This book was runner-up for the Newbery Medal in 1968.

Fattypuffs and Thinifers

ANDRÉ MAUROIS

Edmund Double loved food and was plump, like his mother, while Terry his brother could hardly wait to leave the table and was consequently very thin, like his father. Nonetheless, they were all very fond of each other and the boys were amazed when, happening by chance to take a moving staircase to the Country Under the Earth, they found themselves split up and thrust headlong into the midst of the dispute between the warring nations of Fattypuffs and Thinifers.

The sparkle and easy humour of André Maurois' book is certain to fascinate children of all ages as long as Fattypuffs and Thinifers co-exist and remain mutually indispensable.

My Friend Mr Leakey

J. B. S. HALDANE

Mr Leakey was the only magician who could bring a sock to life, or bewitch a tie-pin and a diary so that he could never lose them. He wanted to run over to Java after lunch, and was going to use a touch of invisibility in the morning to cure a dog that was always biting people.

If you want to know more about Mr Leakey and his household jinn and the octopus who served his meals and the dragon (wearing asbestos boots) who grilled the fish, you must read this book to find out.

For readers of eight and over, especially boys.

A Pony in the Luggage

GUNNEL LINDE

It all began when Aunt Tina insisted on taking her nephew and niece on a trip to Copenhagen. And she managed splendidly, even when Nicholas helped an old gentleman off the train with two suitcases belonging to someone else, and the children developed their eccentric passion for visiting the zoo. (How could she guess that they intended to win a pony in a lottery?) Even at the hotel, when people in the room below began complaining of stamping and jumping noises on the ceiling, she didn't guess that there really was a pony in the children's bedroom, or that they were planning to keep it hidden from her until they got it safely home.

A hilarious story by a prizewinning Swedish author which keeps you laughing and wondering to the very end. For readers of eight and over, whether they love ponies or not.

If you have enjoyed this book and would like to know about others which we publish, why not join the Puffin Club? You will receive the club magazine, *Puffin Post*, four times a year and a smart badge and membership book. You will also be able to enter all competitions. For details of cost and an application form send a stamped addressed envelope to:

The Puffin Club, Dept. A
Penguin Books Limited
Bath Road
Harmondsworth
Middlesex